I0836767

CADENZAS
a work of fiction

Alex Kuo

REDBAT BOOKS PACIFIC NORTHWEST WRITERS SERIES

CADENZAS

a work of fiction

ALEX KUO

redbat books
2021

CADENZAS

First Edition: November 9, 2021

ISBN 978-1-946970-06-0
Library of Congress Control Number: 2021949133

Published by
redbat books
La Grande, OR 97850
www.redbatbooks.com

IMAGE CREDITS—cover: *The Goldberg Variations*, Bach (C.F. Peters); pg. 5: Charles Olsen photo by Juangris (CC BY-SA 4.0), *Cao Xueqin* by Mankong (CC BY-SA 4.0); pg. 15: *Smith Corona Silent typewriter* by P. Musgrave (CC BY-SA 3.0); pg. 24: *Scaevola taccada-with Albatross foot prints in sand-Frigate Point Sand Island-Midway Atoll* by Foest and Kim Starr (CC BY 3.0 U.S.), *Whitetail track* by Jim Thomas (CC BY-SA 3.0); pg. 27: Fritz Kreisler *Three Cadenzas*, Beethoven (C.F. Peters); pg. 28: AP Photo/Frank Augstein; pg. 40: Beethoven's First Violin Sonata (C.F. Peters/sheet music: mfiles.co.uk); pg. 45: *Dancing bear in Bulgaria* by Bin im Garten (CC BY-SA 3.0); pg. 48: *Lockheed EP-3E Orion (ARIES II), USA - Navy* by Pedro Aragão (CC BY-SA 3.0); pgs. 54, 55, and 56: *Cello Concerto No. 1*, Shostakovich (International Music Company); pg. 62: *Tank Man Rubber Duckies* from Sina Weibo (weibo.com); pg. 64: *Tank Man* by Jeff Widener of The Associated Press; pg. 66: *Ivo Pogorelich at the Metropolitan Museum of Art* Photo credit: Nan Melville for The New York Times; pg. 67: Beethoven's First Violin Sonata (C.F. Peters/sheet music: mfiles.co.uk); pgs. 68 and 69: *Piano Concerto No. 2*, Prokofiev (Breitkoph & Hartel); pg. 72: Cover of T*he Defense* by Vladimir Nabakov (edition: published by Vintage, 1990); pg. 73: Cover of *Mao's Kisses* by Alex Kuo (redbat books, 2019); pg. 74: *2007 Venice Cup Winners* credit: Swan Game; pg. 75: Chicago Daily Tribune Headlines—September 23, 28-29, 1920; pg. 76; First Edition cover of *The Natural* by Bernard Malamud (Harcourt, Brace and Company, 1952), Wonderboy bat (thegoldencloset.com); pg. 78: Milstein sisters photo by Marco Borggreve; pg. 79: Cover of *Swann's Way* by Marcel Proust (Penguin Classics, Revised edition, 2004), Cover of *Doctor Faustus* by Thomas Mann (Alfred A. Knopf, 1948); pg. 83: Cover of *a* by Andy Warhol (Grove Press, 1968), Cover of *Z* by Vassilis Vassilikos (edition: published by Nosso Tempo, 1975); pg. 85: *Brandenburg No. 5*, Bach (Barenreiter); pg. 97: *The Goldberg Variations*, Bach (C.F. Peters).

Printed in the United States of America.

Text set in Garamond Premier Pro

Book design by
Kristin Summers, redbat design | www.redbatdesign.com

One should never write a book until he is on his deathbed, because he won't live to regret it.

—Tsien Hsue-shen, cyberneticist

Survivors are perpetrators of lies.

—Zoe Filipkowska, writer, photographer

Every era puts invisible shackles on those who have lived through it, and I can only dance in my chains.

—Liu Cixin, *The Three-Body Problem*

1

At first a few of them survived the classroom's filibuster and then later, the censor's bonfires. For the most part they now bunch together on our maps as hot stars, and sometimes some of them can be seen and measured with Hubble's infrared spectroscope. Depending on the precise axial rotation of the sun and making allowances for the stalking Doppler effect, a careful squint at these shrouds can be recorded to expand the spectrum of our nebulous coordinates.

When that translation happens, we call it fiction.

This is just the way this book is going to go.

As a reader, you may ask what is the origin of this book? The answer may sound absurd, and stone, cold boring. But then, we've already come this far. Let's get on with it.

Once in the village of La Mancha, there lived this spare man bordering on fifty with indistinct features named Alonso Quijano. [PROOFREADER'S NOTE: literary scholars have disagreed on the accuracy of this name, some believing that the author had used a pseudonym to protect him.] Whatever. The meeting that evening started with a dinner of lentils and boiled mutton.

So when there were enough to fill all the ballots in the room, Aria embraced the particulars and stood up. Believe me, he said, it all happened so very fast no one knew for sure it wasn't an act of the imagination. *Count them*, he cautioned, *count them to be sure this isn't something we'll find in tomorrow's papers.*

We did just as he had asked, signing each piece of paper folding all our signed promises of secrecy. There was no collusion or dissension.

In a special edition the next morning, the opposition printed the story anyway, and it included names of all the authors who had signed the ballots, including dates and places for the most part as truthfully as possible.

Aria called just before the story first came out on twitter, then later on television. *We have been betrayed*, he said, *we had all promised to be silent, but someone has betrayed us.* I tried to tell him it'll be all right, they had no proof, no corroborating evidence to make them credible, the republic will not panic.

But Aria reminded us we didn't have any either—yet we believed these disappearances had occurred like before, much as we often place our trust in random coincidences and wild repetitions and in fact have come to expect them like children. Then he disappeared entirely, his voice trailing into thin air.

By the time of the emergency council meeting that afternoon, only six of us showed up. We idled at one end of the long conference table trying to reconstruct the notes bar by bar, repeating them again and again, trying to be sure we had not left out any note, any note at all, past all the etymology and extracts.

So who are these people who decipher and analyze the measurements of this stellar matter and transcribe them into the book that we hold in our hand while avoiding the stale debris of old truths? Here are some examples, although such random selections may only be further misleading, as anecdotes often are, like a parable or metaphor. But at this moment there is nothing else to rely on, no probability table crunched from sustainable data entries. This is all we've got for now.

In the liner notes, the author had lied and changed his name to Cervantes and moved to Madrid at the beginning of the 17th century to document something quixotically funny that no reader, editor or publisher could identify with. But no matter, its many pages would slowly appear in print, serially at first and then they kept on reappearing for hundreds of years later in one hundred fifty languages under the title name of its main character.

Correction. Strike that. He might have changed his name to Cow a century or so later and wrote *The Story of the Stone*, even though he had never been to Beijing, or China, for that matter, and did not understand a word of its curly Mandarin, written or spoken.

The original manuscripts of these two books can now be found in the Natural Bibliotica of the Mind on Pizzumo in Buenos Aires, where Sotheby's had auctioned off some of the Third Reich's plundered treasures of paintings, sculptures, jewelry, in order to bolster their legal defense against the charges of theft and crimes against humanity. This library is open now seven days a week. During weekday mornings before noon, there, one can see the publicist, the slim archivist director, airbrushed in a photoshop parlor, square-jawed and khaki uniformed with spit-shined, brass-studded shoulder epaulets and a matching eye-scanned entry card hanging from his neck, ready to give you a tour but, please, oh please, do not touch, do not turn the pages, don't even breathe on them. And close the door behind you, please.

In addition to these manuscripts, this library had cobbled together five rogue photos in passport size of those who had attended the emergency council meeting four paragraphs back, even when the narrative text that has survived a legion of agents, censors and proofreaders mentioned six. Someone is missing. Can you guess who?

But on closer look, one of these five does not belong to the original six:

1. Who is he? Someone undercover to incite chaos, or just a writer pilfering notes down to the last detail just in case he can't remember it for his next novel?
2. Our technicians were not able to find any physical match for him, not even anything close in its colossal biometric iris scan data bank. In other words, there are two missing, with a walkin inserted just to muddy the search.
3. The author has double-counted the narrator and Aria as two separate persons, so that the accusation of betrayal would be directed to the *nom de guerre*, the imagined Aria.
4. And, just maybe, the narrator, Aria, and the author are the same person.

   Your turn. Fill in the blanks below.

Name of top left: ______________________________

Was he at the meeting? ______________________

Name of top right: ____________________________

Was he at the meeting? ______________________

Name of next left: ____________________________

Was he at the meeting? ______________________

Name of next right: ___________________________

Was he at the meeting? ______________________

Name of last: _________________________________

Was he at the meeting? ______________________

Who are the two missing? _______________________

Do you care? _________________________________

What about the author, narrator, and Aria: are they the same person? Then if not, are two of them the same person? If so, who is the one out? Each one has an equal chance of being the one out. Unless, of course, there is that fabulous chance that every one of the three is imagined. In which case, we the readers will just have to accept things as they are and not try to change them, shearsman that we're not.

Next, an examination of our nebulous coordinates.

Cadenza: Latin for improvisation, riff, a cloud of musical notes, weightless in its projective field where the line begins on the left. Or is it on the right? Like ionized gases, they vary in size from a single utterance by the recent Sonny Rollins on tenor sax, to Ludwig van Beethoven one-hundred-and-fifty years ago, whose two *cadanze* for Wolfie Mozart's piano concerto in D minor cascaded into one-hundred-and-eleven bars barely tolerant of the initial aria. From a simple sentence, to a complete chapter. And even then it ain't over until the fat lady sings, of songs no longer heard, and of books not remembered.

It's Aria again, *da capo*, return to the beginning again, a cloud of notes twittering on G, his key for most of his encrypted messages. *What happened is not an act of the imagination*, he said, and repeated it, *not an act of the imagination. Not at all*, he whispered the reiteration, as if it were a treasured secret kept from the marauding authority.

We must hide it from the censors and believers of all sorts, he cautioned, as they would surely get it wrong and misrepresent it while they ask for it to be played again or not at all in their sleepless nights in Leipzig and much later in Morocco, 1942. Then he asked each of us to swear our promise to secrecy and protect those writers whose language was competent and stable, but whose vocabulary was actually quite mundane and often ponderous in order to accurately represent the tedious rhythms and the invisible shadows of most of our lives most of the time, where the fragility of this language attempts to combine form and content and ignore the software limits of the beginning-middle-and-end.

Who really gives a fuck how the cat got up the tree and how it got back down, our translator added.

Look at J.S. Bach's *Goldberg Variations,* he gave as an example by texting us its cover. Bach and his Nürnberg publisher had marketed it in 1741 as a keyboard exercise for instruments with two keyboards. Like a careful novelist, he used a repeated and mundane harmonic bass line by starting each note of the aria and every one of all its thirty variations with a G in the left hand except for the last, marked a disputed *quodlibet,* appearing as the second note in the left hand, a sustained half note.

Aria ended this call with the following notation: while it appears that form and content more easily coalesce in musical compositions than in writing, especially novels, it sets up another equation when the performer is introduced, the intermediary, the translator, without whom the music does not exist, at least not to most of us. The Goldberg has been recorded more than two hundred times, from Wanda Landowska to Jeremy Denk, from Tatiana Nikolayeva to Igor Levit, Mirjana and John Lewis, and then there is of course that eccentric pianist from Toronto, Glenn Gould on his Steinway CD318, and his nearly blind tuner Verne Edquist.

That left us with another question: has the performer then become the form, and the music score the content, or the other way around? Or has that question only become an ordinal issue for the attentive listener or the discerning reader?

The marked time signature in a musical score can change dramatically to the experienced ear that faults the hubris of time as determined chronologically by the beginning, middle, or end, especially in a narrative such as a novel. Within the nebula of multi-dimensional string theory, time in its four dimensional nebulum becomes relative, in the process gaining additional properties that include the Möbius revolutionary cycle in which a moment in time can be overlapped and repeated time and again, utterly

$$\chi\,(\mathrm{u,v}) = (1 + \tfrac{v}{2}\cos\tfrac{u}{2})\cos \mathrm{v}$$

$$\mathrm{y(u,v)} = (1 + \tfrac{v}{2}\sin\tfrac{u}{2})\sin \mathrm{u}$$

$$\mathrm{z(u,v)} = \tfrac{v}{2}\sin\tfrac{u}{2}$$

destroying the concept of beginning, middle and end, making it possible to have a memory of the future inhabiting a moment of an imagined past. Within that configuration of time, then, did the cat ever go up the tree? Or, if it did, did it ever come down? Or did the cat start by being up in the tree in the first place?

Such deliberate examination of the scale of our language takes for granted that words matter. Just maybe no word is that transparent or important in all of its chromatic fantasies.

Where the line begins on the left is another matter altogether. Breaking the hierarchical chains of traditional education, in 1933 a group of American educators opened a collective school in North Carolina and named it Black Mountain College. Emphasizing an interdisciplinary and experimental approach with emphasis on the arts, the college did not hold formal classes, and became a precursor to such schools as UC at Santa Cruz in California, Marlboro in Vermont, Shimer in Illinois, Roger Williams in Rhode Island, and Evergreen in Washington. It eliminated all curricular requirements and grades, dismissed classes, and everyone in residence was expected to participate in cultivating the campus, from tilling the farm to peeling the potatoes in the kitchen.

In the transformative and creative space the college provided before it ran out of gas in its short longevity of twenty-four years, it gathered such radical residents as John Cage and Buckminster Fuller, Josef and Anni Albers, Gwendolyn Knight and Franz Kline, the deKoonings and Robert Rauschenberg, Mary Richards and Merce Cunningham, and its visiting lecturers included Albert Einstein and William Carlos Williams.

And there were no lines on campus, that is, not until the poet and essayist Charles Olson came along as the rector of the college in 1956 and started talking trash about the philosophy of writing poetry, and then publishing it, as if everyone was paying attention, uh-huh. There he is, in that portrait of him in Chapter  with his chin resting on his left hand, caught in a rare moment with his mouth shut before ordering the line for questions to form to his left. Or was it to his right?

In what his supporters claim as the manifesto for the Black Mountain poets movement—whatever a movement is—he introduced the topic of *projective verse*, essentially proclaiming how organic poetry should be written to get away from the debilitating shrines of conventional and academic poetry. To be free, poetry must be written in an open field in which it goes from the head to the ear and then to the syllable, he said, and from the heart to the breath and then to the line. And above all, the length of each line should be determined by the breath of the poet rather than a conventionally predetermined meter, he added, later crystallized by Robert Creeley: *form is never more than an extension of content.*

The American poets who accepted his invitation to join this mixed-media collage included Robert Creeley, Robert Duncan, Denise Levertov, and Gary Snyder, and the group became identified as the Black Mountain Poets, until Olson himself exposed it: this *whole* Black Mountain Poet *thing is a lot of bullshit*, in a National Poetry Myth month when he was accused of white male imperialism and misogyny.

Just maybe artists should refrain from talking and writing about their work, be they dancers, pianists, painters or writers. It can only get them into more trouble.

Since he had no desire to remember the name of the village that was home to the character he made up named Alonso Quijano, the closest the sixteenth/seventeenth century Spanish author Miguel de Cervantes came to identifying it was the agricultural La Mancha region around the coordinates of 30°North and 4° West. A spare man with gaunt features and a great sportsman, he stayed up nights reading romances until they addled his mind and, like a viral contagion, infected his soul as well. He abandoned his silk doublets, velvet breeches and shoes to match for the holidays and dedicated the rest of his life to the role of a knight-on-an-errand, restoring chivalry and easily slipping into the heroic madness of saving himself and his country.

Actually, it's madness what writers will go through to make up the personalities of their characters in their pages of fiction. A little remembered detail from here and there, something read or seen in a movie, sometimes something entirely made up, something borrowed, something stolen, something broiled medium rare.

And so here it comes.

The first thing Cervantes had to do was change the name of Alonso Quijano to the more distinguished Don Quixote de la Mancha. Next, Don Quixote had to have a terrific young horse with a reliable name that didn't eat too much and obeyed commands, which DQ renamed Rocinante. Then of course he had to find someone smart enough to attend to all his needs, including keeping his lance in shape. With the promise of giving him a governorship, he found a farm hand with another made-up name, Sancho Panza, and mounted him on a sturdy donkey named Dapple for their journey.

The challenges of separating reality and its representation circulate throughout this early novel, not only for Cervantes writing the narrative, but for the characters themselves. The stories Don Quixote and Sancha Panza hear on their journey become their stories, and they become agents and writers participating in reshaping their own cameo histories. At certain crucial points in this episodic novel whose different scenes can be shuffled into any order, the reader is tempted to join the horse and donkey parade searching for their author.

No, Cervantes did not change his name to Cow, but another writer with a similar sounding name did, Cao Xueqin, who lived near Beijing a century later, though he was born 200 leagues away in Nanjing. And actually, living in eighteenth century China, he was conversant in both the northern plains Beijing Mandarin curly dialect, as well as Nanjing's southern harsher and less-rounded version. He spent a decade writing *The Story of the Stone* in vernacular Chinese, with the manuscript in some eighty chapters unfinished on his sudden death in 1763 and, with an additional forty chapters from notes and edited by his painter friend Gao E, it was not published until thirty years later.

Which could happen to writers back then who lived in Beijing and drank too much cheap rice wine, or now to those who are shackled when they disturb the State Administration of Press and Publication's watchful censors.

Located in an enormous mansion in an imagined Beijing, this novel describes in excruciating detail the social and financial interaction and tension of an extended family and their servants, in the process revealing their privileged daily lives in the trifling and manicured but strict hierarchy of manners in which a wrongly-placed pair of chopsticks or a careless utterance would have dire consequences. With a cast of hundreds, they whiled away their hedonistic lives in sumptuous dinners and lavish parties, trading domestic gossip, listening to some melody on a qin or pipa, playing complicated board games, and participating in the poetry club that was scheduled to meet weekly.

With some encouragement and funding from the family elders, the poetry club decided to invite an internationally renowned commentator to be the judge of the season's finale of its highly competitive poetry workshop sessions just before the autumn moon celebrations. They decided to ask the American Rush Limbaugh, the recent recipient of the American Presidential Medal of Freedom, who readily accepted and had in fact begun taking notes of this event for his next book. As a safety precaution, the club also invited the correspondent and writer of this work of fiction, Alex Kuo, and helped him get through the tight customs inspection for his Smith Corona Silent typewriter

which he needed to record everything said or unsaid as truthfully as possible.

Oddly enough, Limbaugh had no trouble with customs when he stepped off his PanAm Sikorsky Flying Boat flight from San Francisco with a duffle bag filled with repackaged Chinese firecrackers that he had planned to resell in China at a jacked up price in order to balance the trade deficit between the two nations.

The dozen finalists were fully prepared for this contest, with the moderator introducing the honorable Mr. Limbaugh, and the correspondent sitting in the back with his Silent typewriter. The poets had their own desks, with identical brush and paper, and ink of the same density prepared equally and distributed by the servants so they would not have to do it. Some of them looked quite young, still in their teens. But the correspondent could tell from their confident postures that from their ten years of intense tutoring in the classics they could recite from rote even the most obscure classical poem on demand and not miss a word.

The instructions were clear, a competition in couplets in sequence, with no restraints on metrics or rhymes. The moderator will begin with a line, and based on a random drawing, the first competitor will add another line to form a couplet before writing a third line which will become the first line of the next competitor's couplet. The only requirements demanded the inclusion of a profound metaphor and reciting the completed lines to the gathering.

Mr. Limbaugh supplied,

> *Last night the north wind blew the whole night through*

To which the first competitor added

> *Today outside my door the snow still flies*

to complete the couplet before composing another line to form the first line of the couplet for the next competitor.

> *On mud and dirt its pure white flakes fall down*

In the back our correspondent could hear someone whisper a snivel about these lines: *No good, no good; I can't under-*

stand a word of it, and he typed it into his typewriter, using the red ribbon for every word of it .

And powered jade the whole earth beautifies
Flakes on the dead plants weave a winter dress

Another said, *That sounds like something written by a trained parrot.*

And on dry grasses gemlike crystalize
Now will the farmer's brew a good price fetch

She's the worst poet in the group, every time the worst. I don't know how she ever made it to the finals.

His full barn to a good year testifies
The ash-filled gauge shows winter's solstice near

Yeah, that metaphor is so profound it'll be sure to confound the reader.

And the frost the river's motion petrifies
Snow settles thickly on sparse willow's boughs

Yucko, she needs more potty training.

In snowbound woods a bough's creek terrifies
The wind-blown snow around the traveler whirls

This is going to be the moment of her life. Pity, pity.

An hour later, the visiting expert Mr. Limbaugh selected these winning lines,

Which, behold in beauty, winter's blasts despise
The hushed yard startles to a cold chough's chatter

before stuffing the cash honorarium into his pocket and rushing to the airport toting his duffle bag filled with the most expensive *Maotai* he could find at the Friendship Store in downtown Beijing.

Into the conventional cadenza in which notes real and imagined are reproduced, writers real and imagined walk into this work of fiction that you are holding. It is Charles Olson's turn to make a cameo for the third time for no reason other than Grove Press publishing his *Call me Ishmael* in 1947. Olson had not made up that title, but Herman Melville used it nearly a century ago as the first line in the third chapter of his one hundred and thirty-five chapter whaling novel *Moby-Dick*. Melville had left most of the story-telling to Ishmael in the first person narrative, except where he walked into the story to provide the necessary backgrounding unavailable to Ishmael, such as in the novel's first two chapters' prequel in which a grammar school teacher and a librarian's assistant laboriously presented a rough history of whaling in the mid-nineteenth century, during which 735 of the global 900 whaling vessels were owned by New Englanders and sailed out of Nantucket, Maine, a whopping 80 percent.

Two thirds of this terraqueous globe are the Nantucketer's, said the omniscient Melville intruding into Chapter 14.

Next, he added, *For the sea is his; he owns it, as Emperors own empires.*

And next, the composer of this cadenza dips my best nib into the inkwell and rewrites the title of Melville's novel:

Moby-Dick: The Hunt of a Lifetime

And, furthermore, convinced that Melville believed that the wish to overwhelm nature lies at the bottom of our hearts, he made up an inscription in quatrains to begin the novel, and repeated it at the end, as if Ishmael had written it twice.

I am a hunt of a lifetime volunteer
Making dreams come true
I am not paid in money, though I have a sponsor
Safari International
I seek not fame or glory, but I am thankful
To be part of the story, I try to make a difference
For we all know what's in store
To light up America and more

At last then, the two hundred ton *Pequod*—with three new masts and embellished with whale body parts, including its captain Ahab's prosthetic leg and its tiller carved from a sperm whale's jawbone—was picked out from Nantucket's Straight Wharf, provisioned for three years, and readied with a fresh crew to set sail for the Pacific by way of the South Atlantic and the Cape of Good Hope on its hunt of a lifetime. Its mission was to return with its hold filled with sperm whale oil for its Quaker owners' ledger, but by now just about anyone who has read an American novel, even in translation, must know that it was actually its captain's revenge voyage for a whale that took his leg, ending in sinking the *Pequod* and killing everyone except the one left to tell the story in his attempt to square the circle.

The western history of the nebulous coordinates must queue from QE I, the Good Queen Bess who ruled over England for almost the entire second half of the sixteenth century, a good hundred years before it gifted its Red Cross to the Union Jack. Under the strict parameters of a steady room temperature and comfortable humidity, Her Highness established legal standards by ordering the construction of physical models for the measurement of volume, weight and distance.

A little more than one hundred and fifty years later, the same process was duplicated in the United States with the support of Washington, Franklin and Jefferson, just before the nation opened up the greatest land sale in history. *Yankee Doodle went to town a-riding on a pony.*

In order to establish some order and structure to this huge land grab and fraud at the end of the nation's Civil War, Congress passed a bill in 1785 authorizing the General Land Office in the Treasury (later as the U.S. Geological Survey within the Department of the Interior) to survey and inventory the nation's public lands so their designated units could be identified, sold, stolen or given away. *Stuck a feather in his cap and called it macaroni.*

The principle methodology mapped the nation's public lands by using measurement units based on the distance of a mile legalized by QE I as 5,280 feet and squared to form a Section of one squared mile of six hundred and forty acres (an acre is based on the English measurements of *rods* and *sur-*

veyor's chains or, more accurately, the size of a plat of arable land that can be tilled by one farmer behind one oxen in one day with a thirty minute lunch break) and located within a Township and Range of thirty-six similar Sections numbered horizontally right to left starting at the top right hand corner and offset against a baseline of North Pole to South Pole principal meridians.

The photographer Minor White once told some students at the La Grande Arts Center in Oregon some eighty years ago that it's the eye that sees the picture, not the camera. He also discouraged the proliferation of the repetitious pretty picture, and thought it should have been left in the acid bath because it did not add anything to our visual landscape.

A few years later one of his students teaching photography at the University of Idaho had come to believe that the mind behind this eye is often filled with linguistic abstractions, a contagious vocabulary of words. The very names of these life forms control what we see and how we see them, like fingers pointing. Sometimes we can't even see it unless we have a lexicon and dictionary to index and explain its existence, often mimicking its symbol and preventing us from experiencing what it really is.

He thought that the most common issue raised by those resistant viewers of abstract paintings such as those by Agnes Martin or Mark Rothko, is coded in their question "But what is it?" What they want is a name or title for the painting, such as *Vase of Tulips*, or *Sunset*, something they can literally relate to. These words do not however exist in total isolation: they are laced with a configuration of inchoate visual fragments, a random pictorial remembrance of images from our imagined past. Together, they form a visual barrier to what the artist actually sees in our natural environment.

One early fall morning he took his equipment down to the Snake River south of the Hells Canyon Dam, on the Idaho side. He wanted to do some representational work with his most reliable 50-mm lens to minimize the lies, and without the blue guitar.

Stepping through a field of Columbia River basalts, volcanic rocks, and billeted metamorphosed ancient ocean floor, along the suture zone between older North America and all of the western United States accreted over 100 million years ago, he took a mental inventory of their composited habitations: pictographs, petroglyphs, mine entrances, inadvertent and deliberate destruction of plants and land forms from hunting, fishing, and camping, evidence of human and horse traffic, as well as water erosion created by the wakes from the excursion and power boats, and, from an old Chinese miners' camp, a Del Monte sardine can dated from the 1930s, during the Great Depression.

Into the second hour of his traverse over this scrum, he noticed an unusual brighter color of sedimentation of hydrated uranium oxides on a large piece of metamorphic rock. He loaded a roll of Agfa Ultra print film into his Nikon F5 and screwed it onto a tripod, focused the lens, and waited a good two hours until the light was just right before pressing the shutter, just once.

For his notebook he copied down the coordinates from his cell phone as 45.635° North and 116.484° West, and from the USFS map in his kitbag he located this rock at the northeast corner of the northwest corner of Section 20, Township 2 North, and Range 51 East.

Back at the parking lot he was greeted by two teenagers in camo yelling and grinning next to their pickup truck with Idaho 1L plates while they loaded their rifles in matching camo, getting ready for their big hunt. Their school had been cancelled to observe the first day of deer season.

Yanker, didel, doodle down, diddle, dudel, lanther, Yanke viver, voover vown, Botermilk und tanther.

There it is, faithfully located in fifteenth century Holland before it was translated into English and adopted as Connecticut's state song five centuries later in the middle of deer season, along with all the buttermilk one could drink.

Believe me, the parched mariner said, and held us with his glittering eye and skinny hand. It all happened so very fast no one knew for sure it wasn't an act of the imagination, he continued. And I was the only one who lived to tell the story; we stood still and listened as three-year-olds. Actually, he said, actually I'm the only one who didn't die, actually creating for us the world of wonderment inhabited by both the not-living and the dead that challenged Beatrice in both *Paradiso* and *Purgatorio*.

We now know that shooting an albatross with a bow isn't exactly the same as

shooting a whitetail deer with a rifle—even though they both end in sadness—but not to the painful depth of our storyteller whose exculpation demanded his periodic confession of his doomed voyage to the South Pole, encountering horrendous winds and waves that make the winter passage through the Bay of Biscay the red sky of a sailor's delight, the *Die Glückliche Zeit* of German submarine wolfpacks attacking the Allied merchant shipping lanes in 1940-42 and successfully sinking nearly nine hundred vessels with five million tons of war materiel.

But by early 1943, the team of military strategists and search theorists came back with what they had been asked to do. Each file they submitted unfolded a series of actionable directives to locate those twelve hundred diesel-powered U-boats that had to cross somewhere in that 130,000 square miles of the Bay on their way to the Allied shipping lanes in the Atlantic, embarking from or returning to their home ports on the west coast of France.

First, bomb these home ports.

Second, since these submarines could not transit submerged for the distance of the Bay, use aircraft to look for the surface wake they leave behind even at periscope depth with decks awash. Train the navigators in the American Lockheed Martin B-24 and PBY Catalina to stick to the five basic search patterns that were developed using the record of previous sightings as a baseline, especially in moments of repetition and boredom. Use them, especially the Square and the Barrier, but allowing some degree of randomness, as some of these German skippers often challenged the rigid hierarchy of their command planners.

And third, above all, audit the German Enigma naval communications, since the code had already been cracked by those Polish mathematicians months before the Luftwaffe's Junkers and Heinkels leveled most of Warsaw in September, 1939. Here, no non-disclosure compact was signed, no promise made to keep it a secret: no collusion or dissension. He did live to tell the story, again and again.

But maybe it all happened so very fast no one knew for sure if was an act of the imagination or the product of what is now acknowledged to be the definitive version written some one hundred years later, this Fritz Kreisler's magical cadenza for Beethoven's violin concerto composed in secret at first, both of them suffering from a hearing loss toward the end of their lives. Such is the pastiche of an unauthorized violin composition project, replacing Beethoven's own furious original that merged the piano and the timpani, much like the project of this novel, whose title had vacillated for months between *Nebulum* and *Cadenza*, finally settling on *Cadenza*s instead of *Cadenze*.

Without form or content, or even any thought of a style to fill the white rectangle of the monitor set at the margins of 1, 1, 1, and 1, and the Georgia font at 12, the project was focused on discovering something without character or plot, and trying to mine something important without a beginning, middle, or end for the serious reader. Without the restraints of content or form, this may as well be written on music paper.

Or the style that stalks every novel, for that matter. Ask Eric Auerbach, Witold Gombrowicz, Primo Levi, Susanne Langer or René Wellek and they might just escape the blabbering on the illusional space between form and content in an imperfect translation, even when James Joyce threw them a sucker punch with his novel about Leopold Bloom in 1922.

Some might say even QE II does a better job when she delivers the Queen's Speech at the annual State Opening of Parliament at the Palace of Westminster, with the 530 carat Star of Africa Cullinan I diamond embedded in the regalic royal scepter, a sign of power, order, and good governance.

As Her Royal Highness sits on the Sovereign's throne and outlines her government's agenda for the coming year, here the reporter and later the translator of this narrative pauses to disturb the text. There is a potential error lurking about, in either the original reporting or a personal judgment in the interpretation of its meaning.

Does a queen sit on a throne, or does she only appear to be sitting when she is actually perching in order to protect the intricate beadwork of her dress?

Does she make a speech, or does she make a pronouncement, as QE I did in 1588 when she commanded the standardization of the yard and other distances?

And what about the veracity of the translator? Our translator is having her own problems with this project. She has very carefully created an anonymity for herself to protect her neutrality and hence the objectivity of her translations. There is no known photograph of her, which is not that easy today when every smart phone has a locator and a camera. But she also does not have a credit card, making it all the more complicated when she tries to rent a car with cash and a fake driver's license that she bought in Kowloon City's underground market before Hong Kong's return to China in 1997. So far she has managed to purchase airline tickets through a third party, pay cash for her lodging, and appear in public looking as forgettable as possible, acting as if she's hiding out in some witness protection program.

But now her work is being challenged by her editor, who is claiming that broadcast videos of the same event show QE II saying something entirely different in her speech.

Look at it here, she said, freezing the frame and pointing to it, this part here, here's where the queen's Kokoshnik tiara almost tottered off her head when she banged her titanium-tipped Excalibur for emphasis when QE II pronounced, *No more memoirs. I hate memoirs. My people will not be allowed to read memoirs. Never again. And mark these words in stone*, whereupon she banged her Excalibur again.

Yes, but, it was only a draft write-up here, a translation, a cadenza ahead of its time, like a memory of the future, a nebulum.

And what is a nebulum, her editor asked.

Something not bound by time, or words.

The translator is like the writer, she added. Both pitiful spies among all the editors and proofreaders or typesetters that have been left behind. A surveillance team to see if there's any serious writer giving away all the secrets that can be used for suicide, just in case it might just come down to just that since the reader has just been defeated by being exposed to too much fraud.

The line must be getting pretty long by now, the editor added, especially when it includes those wannabe writers wanting to produce best-selling memoirs lined up on the left.

But there is also that other line, that line on the right; but it is getting thin, when these writers are serious about separating what is believed from what is true, and how the censor hidden inside each and every one of us will nudge us to be social and play it safe and say nothing: do not disturb the equilibrium of the republic.

And who are they then, the editor finally asked after a long pause.

That will depend on where we position that line. In the sand? On a map? Inside an idea? On a dare? Here're a dozen, whose politics are grounded in life and not in something as lovely as a tree.

Claribel Alegría
Maya Angelou
Emily Dickinson
Carolyn Forché
Joy Harjo
June Jordan
Maxine Hong Kingston
Carolyn Kizer
Denise Levertov
Audre Lorde
Joyce Carol Oates
Adrienne Rich

Aria called just before the story came out. Politics, he said, politics is what connects everyone to the world around us, but most of the time we are betrayed by their words that have lost their meaning, whose reiteration in the memoirs of their writers become the social glue adhering one generation to another while pledging allegiance to say nothing.

But into this nebula on this side of the Milky Way, someone will occasionally appear and talk to us, whose work will stray from the program and find a new language to disturb the book clubs. One of them is the Han poet and revolutionary of swords and explosives, Qiu Jin, where a statue remembering her can be found at West Lake, outside Hangzhou, China.

Qiu had committed her life to fighting for gender equality and against the Manchus and the ruling Qing government.

漫云女子不英雄，
萬里乘風獨向東。
詩思一帆海空闊，
夢魂三島月玲瓏。
銅駝已陷悲回首，
汗馬終慚未有功。
如許傷心家國恨，
那堪客裡度春風。

Don't tell me women are not the stuff of heroes
I alone rode over the East Sea's winds for ten
thousand leagues
I grieve to think of the bronze camels, guardians
of China, lost in thorns
Ashamed, I have done nothing; not one victory
to my name
I simply make my war horse sweat
So tell me; how can I spend these days here

The Qing government troops finally caught her in 1907 and beheaded her in Shaoxing (30 miles from West Lake) at the age of 31.

A century later, the Han government of the Chinese Communist Party under the presidency of Xi Jinping, incarcerated more than a million Uyghurs, Kazakhs, and Kyrgyz and other Muslims in re-education camps in northwest China near its border with Tibet.

The rest of us had to wait one hundred and eleven years for her words to survive before *The New York Times* would run a belated obituary for Qiu Jin.

The thing is, often writers are so fixated on the historical accuracy of their work that they leave out the truth. Most of the time there isn't a choice, but once in a while there is. Dante had to make some choices in his *Divine Comedy* seven hundred years ago. Pope Nicholas III kept his name in the Eighth Circle of Hell, and Dante's teacher Brunetto Latini kept his in the Seventh Circle, while the woman he admired kept hers as she wandered around freely in *Paradiso,* as did Dante as a walkin throughout the long poem.

We have come to expect alternate realities as real things, even though we do not have any evidence to make them credible. Like that time when the hunting guide got out of his pickup at the Trailways depot, still thinking about what an anonymous Tehran woman had said in an interview for a magazine piece he read earlier that morning: *I have come to regard men and violence as inseparable.* He thought about the wolf and how its body had been torn apart bone by bone, from the *metatarsal* to the *sesamoid* to the *tarsal* hanging on the barbed wire fence in every township and range in the American west. From the *Canis lupus* to the elk now, wapiti, *Cervus canadensis,* its head mounted and hanging in restaurants at truckstops on Interstates 70, 80, and 90 all the way west to the Pacific Ocean from the Mississippi River. Then bang, a door slammed shut next to him, and everything simply evaporated, bones and all.

An obese woman had shut the door at the bus terminal, and stood next to him now starting to wave a hand at the first passenger stepping off the bus, a troll of bracelets gnarling down her raised flabby arm, a cigarette in the other. The three of them looked at each other, standing there on the same piece of pavement between Interstates 80 and 90, 300 miles from the Pacific. Must be her son, looking like a pvt in civvies returning from basic, barely old enough to have graduated from high school, a young boy stuffed into the body of a man with baseball hat. And this didn't just happen anywhere, not in Madrid, Buenos Aires, Casablanca, Black Mountain, Warsaw, Beijing or Nantucket, but right there in downtown Lewiston, Idaho.

The next to step down was the young guest from Freedom, Pennsylvania, but he looked much older after months of chemotherapy for terminal Hodgkin's. Hair cut short to the stubble like the pvt's, loose in Cabela's overstock of desert camos in tank top, pants, boots, and watch-strap, dressed for his Hunt of a Lifetime. The guide walked up to the boy and tugged on his matching camoed rifle case and duffel bag and called him, *John*?

The boy was speechless, finally asking, *you're my hunting guide, what*? *You're my hunting guide? Funny name, G. G stands for what*?

G was patient, this kid's got only a few months left to live, for chrissakes. Yes, me heathen Chinee no play poker here in Idaho six generations, name means double trouble or dragon eater, whatever.

John wanted to see the town a little the next morning, starting at the airport where he identified the mounted Lockheed F-80 Shooting Star, yes, right, a Korean War veteran clouded in silver and returned from the Peruvian Air Force in a lend-lease reversal and gifted to Lewiston.

And what do they do around here, John pointed to a couple of men handing out free red bibles outside a high school.

They go to karaoke bars, rodeos and monster truck rallies. Be nice G, be nice. They trash evolution and climate change, good country people unburdened by humility mercy or books. And they watch football and they hunt and kill everything.

It's pretty much the same in Freedom, John said, just thirty minutes from the Pirates, Penguins, and Steelers, and the foundation that grants hunting adventures to children with terminal illnesses. *But it'll make my dream come true,* furrows gathering on his forehead and trying to forget the sickness in his lungs and liver and the months of radiation that seared his hair and took away his flesh.

At the entrance to the city park a reader board offered free pizza and a pitcher of beer to successful hunters who've shot a wolf in the open season that started with the Lewis and Clark expedition two centuries ago, the ongoing blood lust annexed to state law just a year ago.

The sunrise was well over an hour away when they came to the end of the dirt road at Little Boulder Creek and parked next to a camper, its back window filled with NRA, Marines and POW-MIA stickers. G flashed the light to the dry creek bed that'll take them most of the way up to the lookout point, about thirty minutes or so, *not too close right behind me, sling your rifle with empty chamber,* the light from his headlamp bouncing as he brushed aside fall's spider webs stretched across the trail, turning around and checking just to be sure John was right with him, hand swatting the light on his face.

They were near the top when the reflection of the glowing sunrise behind McGary Butte silhouetted the saddle along the ridge line where they took a rest and waited until it was light enough to believe what they were seeing in the emerging landscape. Boxed lines here to demark the boundary of a BNSF clearcut, a color there separating ponderosas from white firs, and the distant shadows slipping over the slope down to the Clearwater in the next township and range. G imagined he could taste the tang of the season's last golden asters above the dust.

It's here, John whispered and handed over the binoculars. *I like him; I like his rack; I like his size and the way he moves.*

It's still a quarter-mile away; we have to get closer.

But John was ready. He had waited months for this moment to kill something. His bolt locked a shell into the chamber of his .308, moving through the dew-covered sage, the elk continuing to graze upwind, oblivious and comfortable in its own domain in the warmth of the gathering sunlight, a set of six-point antlers showing when they were 200 yards out. Prone, John peered into his scope until the black dot centered on the elk at a point up from the front leg and just back of the shoulder for a lung and heart shot in this perfect hunt he had dreamed about and practiced for in which he carried his own rifle, squeezed the trigger and did his own killing, and wham, the Winchester 180 grain Black Talon hollow point bullet twisting out of the 24-inch barrel and into the target at more than 2,000 foot-pounds, its recoil slamming back into his shoulder.

G waited a moment before he ran to the downed elk with its forelegs twitching and chest still heaving, and to end the searing pain ripping into the bull's lungs and flesh, he quickly snapped the safety off his own rifle and fired a shot straight into the elk's head just behind the occipital bone facing him, killing him instantly, first for the elk, then for the boy, then for the rest of us, dead or alive, wanted or not.

Next, a picture was taken of the kneeling John for his keepsakes. Another for the foundation. A third for the *Lewiston Tribune*.

The next day G helped John with the duffle and rifle case at the bus depot. Hunt of a Lifetime paid a local taxidermist to shoulder-mount the elk head and picked up the shipping charges to Pennsylvania for the 200 pounds of custom cut-and-dry-iced flesh connected to it. John left town still a young boy who had just made his choice to take a life, just as his own would be taken from him before Christmas without his choice.

At the last recital, a series of notes between the piano and violin collided until the violin's sustained high note toward the end of the sonata's exposition was held for two bars without intervals to interrupt its meaning, clear and significant, as if waiting for an impromptu cadenza or riff without a fermata 𝄐 marking in the score, as if a curtain had been raised to change the program notes forever. Folded into the disgruntled literacy of the state-owned-and-operated telecaster counting the number of people in the concert hall with sandalwood-scented fans, and small opera glasses who had arrived early by Uber or any other consumer pairings of utilitarian interest to corporate sponsors, the two musicians occasionally glanced at each other for any complication in time signature or clarity in note articulation, with the inconspicuous page turner glued to the pianist's left where the line forms, as always.

Both the edited score and the program notes had listed this piece as a violin sonata, directing the casual listener's ear to its slashed and burned quavers at stage center, especially when the violinist was performing on another stolen Stradivarius recently recovered by the F.B.I.

It's also not something one can tap one's foot to, in the beginning, middle or end of this sonata. But in listening to it, or at least most of the time, some of us were slowly assimilating to this language's clichés, even when the writer had fervently rejected them in the first place. These are some of the consequences a writer and a composer have to live with, like it or not. We imagine what we hear, and music becomes the allegory of our life, as if remembering something we did not fully understand, or like this novel that could well end at any moment, like Joseph Haydn's F#-minor symphony, with the musicians leaving with their instruments, each note decaying one by one in the farewell.

It must be about the same for numbers, at least natural numbers because they cannot be made into symbols, metaphors or parables to confuse us. The use of these numbers in a mathematical trick to tease out the way space curves in field equations of motion actually directed Albert Einstein to a theory about gravitational pull of black holes and a Nobel in 1921. But while much of his work took place at the Prussian Academy of Sciences in Berlin in the 1910s, the actual discovery took place when he accepted a research residency for a couple of years in Brazil in the 2010s when the light from the sun was bent by earth's gravitational pull, causing a warping of the space/time continuum.

When that mammoth 13-million-digit prime number got to Brazil, its president took the key to its capital Brasília and opened the vault to distribute free circus tickets to everyone. Aerialists hung from the rafters of the Rio de Janeiro Opera House and sang their favorite song, cheered on by an overflow crowd of well-wishers larger than the opening for the 2014 FIFA World Cup or the 2016 Summer Olympics. For days, trained zebras and lions that had promised not to attack their trainers accompanied the 7.13 megabyte number through the residential neighborhoods and offered chocolates to those who had flunked high school algebra now gathered at street corners gawking at the long string of hostile digits,

$$2^{43112609} - 1$$

...470,269,330,255,923,143,453,723,949,337,516,054, 106,188,475,264,644,140,304,176,732,811,247,493,069, 368,692, ...

The series started with 2, 3, 5, 7, 11, 13, 17, 19, 23, 29, 31, 37, 41, 47, 53, plump real numbers that can only be divided by themselves and 1. The trumpeting elephant assured us that they form the basic blocks of natural numbers, and don't you forget it. You can't even look up the daily Dow, Nasdaq or S&P 500 without the help of these primes. Competing to keep its readers from defecting to text, tweet, stream, or post, the leading newspaper *Journal de Brasil* conducted a daily contest with a one-million-autographed-Mao-Tse-tung-¥ reward for the first reader to text in the correct number for the daily, three-digit, prime number with the published entry password in Portuguese.

Those with double-liens on their homes had to ante up a spontaneous autobiographical disclosure about their mathematical shortcomings or face closure. Face it, they had failed, in grade school and in high school, and for whatever reason—inattention, had skipped breakfast that day, plain lazy, or just didn't give a shit. Time to ask and tell. Did you fuck up in third grade arithmetic, thereby ending any further learning except to tell time and count change backwards at the checkout register? Can you balance your bank account? Can you tell a Canadian loonie from an American quarter? Can you tell a crow from a raven? And finally, can you tell a Crow from a Blackfeet when they both live on Hollywood Boulevard?

Einstein joined the mathematics professors at the fancy University of São Paulo when they objected to using a network of 75 linked Dell desktop computers at UCLA to generate this new, 46th Mersenne prime number. That's cheating, like asking for divine tutelage. And then you dare come down here dragging that useless twenty-eight mile-long number across the equator behind you, boastful and arrogant? North, your default orientation, north, that doesn't even exist down here. *Nada, nada.* The knife thrower never misses.

Listen, it's not really that big of a deal, if you have enough computers and enough time and enough interest. We don't even have any use for these numbers past the first thousand that ends in 7919, except for some computation shortcuts in information technology systems that handle vast data streams, and in some code work for government and corporate espionage. And besides, the list of these basic, natural numbers is infinite. Just look at Euler's proof of the infinitude of primes:

$$\sum_{prime} \frac{1}{p} = \frac{1}{2} + \frac{1}{3} + \frac{1}{5} + \frac{1}{7} + \frac{1}{11} + \ldots = \infty$$

By now the patient clown with the red nose and the balloons had time enough to join us and started searching the crowded streets for irony. He found an American hiding in the white space between house numbers holding a winning raffle ticket for a collectible convertible with fins, but he's not sure if the man's from the north or the south, or if he's just lucky. He released the blue balloon on a street corner he can't reveal because he had worked for the CIA in the seventies, just in case. The magician walking besides him coaxed him into letting go of the other balloons as well, and children dashed madly after them, took daring risks, and jumped the gap from rooftop to rooftop over the streets' hard skin below them. They didn't care, they've scraped their knees before, and they were convinced the balloons will give them space for glee and smiles.

In the afternoon the Magic Markers marching band led by Flora Purim and trick riders, accompanied by the Four Mad Mammas who formed a huge quartet of bouncing red capital Ms

stretched across the entry promenade to Rio's Museum of Natural History, projecting sonic joy without any fault in count, pitch, timbre or voice. The dancing in the streets was led again by the president singing and clapping along and giving out babies to same-sex couples until well after midnight. What was not obvious at the time: several digits from the 46th Mersenne prime had taken furlough from the line, and joined the celebration camouflaged as indiscriminate and random letters from the user-friendly alphabet which no one questioned, even when they guessed at the meaning of words they had not seen or heard before or had forgotten. But to this day no one knows for sure the exact location of these digits' point of departure from the line, and if they all returned to their original positions, or if anything had been altered or damaged by their temporary absence. Time will tell, but only with the help of giant primes; if it's going to take some time for this question to be remembered without ambiguity.

Here, however, is where we run into trouble. What is ambiguity? In what language is it articulated? English? Portuguese? What is the mother tongue here? If it's accompanied by irony, it'll definitely complicate these questions. And then what about intention, or symbol, metaphor or parable? Who are you asking, the monkey with the organ grinder, or the dancing bear?

The thing itself or the meaning of the thing? That 19th century Danish thinker had something to say about this, if only our language can capture and retain the thing and its essence and not alter it, or something like that. Maybe the answer lies with numbers, they'll get it right, no doubt about that. But then again, maybe life's more fun with ambiguity, no?

Well you see then, your ticket's all punched out, the show's over for you. If you want to go through this again, you'll just have to follow the number to Argentina to catch its next show. They play better bridge down there. Your Spanish won't be a problem, since you were so good at faking Portuguese here. But don't take my word for it. See that guy there sitting down at the court house steps by the tail end of the number? That's the Ringmaster, and he's taking all this down on a yellow legal pad so we won't forget, see? Go talk to him, he'll tell you if this isn't just another one of those stories we inhabit. Call him Einstein.

The music score was never entirely blank, but splattered with spilled ink and a mélange of notes as if we know the history of how and when each of them came into our life and has since acquired a familiarity that challenges our memory. The same for the canvas that was never white to begin with, its flecks of drying latex paint, never plain white to begin with, or the paper loaded into our printer just waiting for the blank white space on the computer in the next room to be filled with enough tiny black pixels to form two-hundred-and-fifty words so that the document could be Wi-Fied to the waiting printer.

For Jerome David Salinger, he started at this beginning then, with the same white pages in his manual typewriter in front of him. But this is hardly an empty space, a space in which the shapes and the writer's intent are constantly changing. Bouquets of parentheses started hurdling out of his notebook, raising high his expectation that the leftover Buddy from a previous story would now take over and try to understand and tell the story of his brother Seymour to unknown readers, pulling imagined snapshots out of his wallet to help him.

And as luck would have it, this Buddy decides that he wants his own story and just ups and walks away with J.D. chasing after him, notebook in hand, each detail stumbling into the next one word at a time until they reach an irreparable and delicate balance.

Into Buddy's story then, we see him as one of the twenty-three in the flight crew on an aerial electronic surveillance flight seventy-miles from China's Hainan Island's Lingshui Naval Base in an Aries II on its return flight to Kadena Air Base in Japan. With a quarter tank of unspent fuel, the pilot had decided to loiter a few more moments trying to suck up any electronic debris to pass off to fleet command as well as submarines in

the vicinity, just long enough to provoke a pair of Chinese J-8 Finback interceptors to

play a cat-and-mouse game with the ferret intruder. The young top gun Finback pilot came in too fast on its second pass at Mach 2 and sheared the Aries II port wing, the shattering sound reverberating backward through the aircraft's entire frame, trashing its number one engine before it spun out of control into a doomed vortex toward the ocean 25,000 feet below.

The Aries pilot had already sent out the Mayday PB-20N Kilo Romeo 919 70 nautical miles SSE of Hainan Island collision with Finback 070 at 22,500 Mayday signal, and the crew followed immediately, declined every number down to zero on every keyboard, slammed the dedicated F12 key three times, manually destroyed the drives on the five laptops on board, and dumped all the operational binders already printed on acetate-treated paper that will dissolve in water into crypto boxes that were shoved out the starboard hatch, before a double check and EDP completed, sir.

The PLA allowed the Aries to make an emergency landing at Lingshui and the crew of the spy plane to stay for the next ten days in the air conditioned military hotel before they were flown out on a Continental Boeing 737 after each crew member was charged $34 for an exit visa out of China, probably forever.

A week later the entire crew appeared at 1600 Pennsylvania Avenue NW where President George W. Bush presented the pilot with the Meritorious Service Medal for leadership, and the Air Medal of a burnished eagle in an attack dive clutching two

lightning bolts in its talons overlaid on two metallic overlapping circular discs hanging from a gold-and-blue ribboned chevron to the rest of the crew. In Beijing Premier Jiang Zemin joined the Central Military Commission in praising PLA Finback pilot Wang Wei as a revolutionary martyr and designated him Protector of the Sea and Sky and called him resolute and daring, cool and calm.

But Salinger was not all done here. His cameo in this chapter comes with his verbatim response to this story that got out of hand. In a forthcoming *Paris Review* interview he said, *What I had left out of the story was a statement made by Vice President Dick Cheney and National Security Advisor Condoleezza Rice: hell, we were just caught and slammed for opening their mail, that's all, even at seventy miles out, well outside the twelve nautical-miles of the international law on territorial boundaries. And besides, they did send us a bill for a two months parking ticket for the Aries at their private Lingshui airport*, which was just enough to save us from using books to wrap barricades around themselves, dancing in our chains.

Aria had cautioned us to be sure it'll not be found in tomorrow's papers, but he was wrong. It did, on August 6 and August 9 anyway, right after the world's first use of WMD that led to the end of World War II and captured by every major newsreel broadcasting company in the world, including Pathé and Movietone News. With that early disclosure which would seem to have erased the necessity of caution, the author of this work of fiction then decided to make a cameo appearance here and address the reader in the third person. As a six-year old he was living in Shanghai's French Concession on those

dates and could have seen the flash of the plutonium 240 implosion at eleven miles high over Nagasaki 500 miles away, even at eleven in the morning, at least according to J.G. Ballard's Jim Graham, who saw it as *an unbroken silence lay over the surrounding land, as if the sun had blinked, losing heart for a few seconds.*

For Kuo, then, he had to wait fifty-three years to find the language and will to describe what it was like for him, a poem under the title of "The Day the War Ended."

I was six the day the war ended in 1945
But I don't remember which flag I waved

There were carnivals everywhere
The regulators were beginning to disappear

The radio station sent out free news
Prison doors opened for fifty today, one hundred tomorrow

One by one they came out, the Red Cross relocating
The head in one place, the feet in another

Most said nothing, others still stood in line
Promising to vote "A" or "A" in the next election

There I am, in that photograph trying to look away
The day the war ended on this street corner

Those others gathered around me were waiting
Blowing out kisses to Movietone News

They lingered, trying to believe whatever happened
That day will not be repeated in anyone's history

Now at more than a half century since that war ended
Our stories are still hedged between hurt and hope

Most of the time I'm watching eyewitness news
As if I'm seeing something taking place in the past

Or between there and here whatever the time
These intolerances have not stopped, whatever the place

This is what it was like exactly that day after
With nothing left to be taken away

Someone is tracing a distant coincidence
Another is doing the same in his head

No one is waiting for messages or decisions
Our fists gripped in ambiguity, between wars

Even a cursory glance at the soloist's first page in the score of Dmitri Shostakovich's Cello Concerto No. 1, would show a simple structure without the nebulous ballots of his Hungarian or Russian contemporaries.

Clear lines of mostly quarter notes and a simple four-note motif that will resonate throughout tomorrow's papers, suggest no need to imagine any malevolent intent.

B$^{\flat}$ut then, this is only the opening of a three story serial, four if we count the six minute cadenza. **C**hord progressions are something else altogether.

A$^{\flat}$ria would remind us not to expect the conventional debris of old truths that have taken over our memory. **B**$^{\flat\flat}$elieve me, he said, listen to his chord progressions. **A**$^{\flat}$nd then he added that we are never quite sure what they are all about and how we got here in the first place, but it's always compelling and convincing, like a work of fiction.

G$^{\flat}$ranted that everyone in the room knew it really wasn't fiction at all, we pretended to go along with it anyway. **B**$^{\flat\flat}$ehind every word of Shostakovich's music lurked the possibility of an imminent arrest, maybe a show trial if he were lucky enough, and then marched off to a Siberian work camp, soap and toothbrush in hand. **E**$^{\flat}$xecution was another possibility, after he was declared an enemy of the people, along with Prokofiev and Khachaturian.

D$^{\flat}$edicating this concerto to his good friend Slava Rostropovich, he decided he needed to come up with a new language for this gift. **C**adenza. Preceded by a lower A on the timpani in double *pianissimo*, it'll have be a long one, starting with something quiet and low but in the following six minutes deplete the vocabulary of the cello and run the scale up to the highest pitch on its left string, the A. These six minutes will scoop up all the musical debris left to the side of the first two movements, the loose notes and dropped phrases, as well as parts of our whispered conversations—heard, unheard or imagined—words that have lost their intended meanings, words that were not meant at all, unfinished sentences, random white noise with no time signature that we use as our social glue to protect us from evil, without which the First Amendment will burn up and we might very well end up in the ninth circle of Dante's inferno.

Believe me, Aria finally said, interrupting again, standing behind the conductor and looking at the text of the cadenza in the teleprompter, granted that the execution of the chord's progressions was even and made sense this time, though they were clearly dedicated to the dominant key. We just sat there and listened, took notes and prepared questions, just before the last seven words in $E^{\flat}$ and double *fortissimo* on the timpani ended and prevented a breathless collision before the applause erupted.

Maybe because it happened so very fast it was indeed an act of the imagination. Just to be sure, we gather now on Zoom for a wireless confirmation in the eternal imperfect tense so it won't challenge the censors poised with their secret daubers as if they're playing Bingo at the Masonic Lodge. Gotcha or not, it's really *the word forms/on the left; you must stand in line* nevertheless.

[EDITOR'S NOTE: that is the correct translation of what was printed in one of Olson's Maximus poems.]

What follows is a slightly edited transcript of the Zoom conversation, carefully transcribed by our author as part of his contract with redbat books and *The Paris Review.*

Gilbert Sorrentino: *I've been asked to moderate this discussion on the art of fiction. But you must know that since I'm from Brooklyn I can't take this subject seriously.*

Henry James: *However, we must take an active interest which in moments of confidence, we may venture to say a little more what it thinks of itself. We must take ourselves seriously for the public.*

Gertrude Stein: *Now listen! I'm no fool. I know that in daily life we don't go around saying is a…is a…is a. But a rose is a rose is a rose, even here in Paris.*

Percy Lubbock: *Well, that depends on your point of view, no?*

György Lukács: *You must already know that I believe the history of the novel is immersed in transcendental homeless-*

ness, characters longing for utopian perfection. This cannot be spoiled by such modernists as James Joyce or Franz Kafka.

Sorrentino: *I'm surprised you didn't include my name in that last sentence.*

Lukács: *Well, as the minister of culture, I try to be fair and polite to everyone.*

Saul Bellow: *Yes, but not everyone is the same. I am Chicago born and I have taught myself, free-style and first to knock. Sometimes innocent, sometimes not so.*

John Gardner: *But we have to be careful here to be sure our best work attempts to test human values to find out which is best to promote human fulfillment.*

Agnes Martin: *I'm very careful not to have ideas, because they are inaccurate.*

[EDITOR'S SECOND NOTE: these writers' work includes *The Art of Fiction, The Craft of Fiction, On Moral Fiction, The Theory of Fiction*, and Agnes Martin works in horizontal lines.]

Sorrentino: *What about you, Mr. Cao, seven thousand miles away there in Beijing. Do you need an interpreter?*

Cao Xueqin: *No thank you, my translator is right here in the studio. I believe the novel's words are not just idle description of the everyday world to help the wine down after a meal with friends. From a good writer, those words make human life more real.*

Jorge Luis Borges: *You and I want the same thing, but we approach it so differently. But that makes sense, since we write more than two hundred years and several languages apart.*

Sorrentino: *Can you say a little more about that?*

Borges: *For example, in one of my stories Paul Menard is a French author whose lengthy bibliography begins with a technical article on how the game of chess can be improved by removing one of the rook's pawns.*

But he is best known for immersing himself in seventeenth century Spanish and completely rewriting, line by line, all thirty-five-plus chapters of Don Quixote before tearing up every draft. The story concludes with the suggestion that only a second Paul Menard would be able to exhume and revise those lost pages light years away from social realism.

James: *If I may be permitted to suggest to our august group of distinguished authors, that it might be supposed if I may help myself out with a French word, naïf, that given our world that is so messy and filled with enormous ambiguities and contradictions, we must find our own way to explore it to its fullest extent and enjoy doing so.*

Larry McMurtry: *I don't know about the rest of you, but I try to keep it simple. For me, there are only two worthwhile plots in all of literature: the stranger comes into town, and the stranger leaves town.*

Margaret Atwood: *Except for the true connoisseur who's only interested in the stretch in between.*

Dorothy Parker: *Given this wide range of gaggles, my best gift to a nephew who wants to be a writer is a loaded pistol.*

Sorrentino: *And what about you, Mr. Roth, with glove on and crouched forward at first base in a game in Iowa City.*

Philip Roth: *Sorry to be abrupt, but I have to concentrate on this next batter. He hits to the right, like Tolstoy. It's our last chance to end the season with a win. Then I have to go back to continue Libby's story. Sorry.*

At this point all the ballots have been filled and the box stuffed.

Sorrentino: *So thank you and that's all folks. Just theme and variations, each chapter bound loosely together by its variation on the same theme. And then there are those like Kafka and Borges; they're on the edge of things and won't take any of this seriously but continue doing what they do best: write.*

Agent, editor, publisher, translator or not, the Zoom conference ended, even though nothing had been confirmed and every line disappeared, real or imagined. Against the best advice of both his publisher and subsidiary agent, in an act of confirmation, the author is insisting on giving the last word to a New Mexico writer.

Simon Ortiz: *If it's fiction, you better believe it.*

Sounding annoyed and a bit distracted, Aria called and said we must release a statement to sustain the readers' confidence in this novel, this work of fiction. We have to come up with someone they can trust, he emphasized, some witness with a reliable memory to make this story that we inhabit compelling and convincing and worthwhile, at least for the moment. We are facing the international media deluge of varying and sometimes conflicting versions of what actually happened in Beijing's political spring of 1989, each with its own self-serving agenda, each one surrounded by a mirage of details, including videos and interviews. *How can facts have meaning, in whatever form*, he asked in desperation. Our work depends on our looking carefully at the content of these facts, what they mean.

So we bent over and carefully scribbled down our nominations on the little squares of paper handed out by the prefect, who collected them, tallied the totals, and announced the popularity: the Tank Man.

This photoshopped image was heisted from one of the three shots taken by Jeff Widener, who, like the other 1,200 journalists and photographers, was assigned to Beijing to cover the historic meeting between Mikhail Gorbachev of the USSR and Deng Xiaoping to mend the Sino-Soviet relationship. [EDITOR'S FACTUAL NOTES: similar photographs were taken that Monday morning, June 5, by Charlie Cole of *Newsweek*, Arthur Wah of Reuters, Stuart Franklin of Magnum, from Beijing Hotel's sixth floor balconies facing west toward Tiananmen Square, over the red hair of a giant Ronnie McDonald in lotus position on the same street, East Chang'an Avenue. Widener of the Associated Press took his photographs–on borrowed film from an exchange student—with a Nikon FE2 camera and a 400 mm lens in Fuji 100 color negative film. Among many awards, this photograph was a finalist for a Pulitzer.]

Surely our readers would think this Tank Man with *Time* magazine's accolade as one of the 100 most important people of the 20th century would be someone whose active witness account would be a reliable narrator.

[MORE EDITOR'S FACTUAL NOTES OF FACT: There are videos of him facing a column of Type 59 main battle tanks from the 1st Armored Division of the 65th Group Army. These tanks were made in Factory 617 in Mongolia and owned by Norinco, short for China North Industries Group Corporation Limited, one of the world's largest military contractors.]

Some rumors have identified him as a nineteen-year old student named Wang Weilin who was charged with political hooliganism, but Chinese officials speaking anonymously, said that their data base was flummoxed by this claim. One of President Richard Nixon's deputy special assistants with the support of PEN International and Hong Kong's Center for Human Rights, made a speech to the President's Club in which he alleged that this Unknown Rebel was executed two weeks later, denied by Politburo member Jiang Zemin, who said *I think never killed*. There have also been reports that this Wang Weilin [sic] was a Peking University graduate student who had too much to drink after his dissertation defense had to be postponed because of the student demonstrations on campus, and just before he was to leave for Taiwan and become a taxidermist at the National Palace Museum. And another that said he was an undercover tank commander trying to realign the tank column to minimize the damage to the old cobbled sections of Tiananmen Square.

Are eyewitness accounts reliable, we asked. Rhetorically, would Lieutenant Colonel George Armstrong Custer be a good source for why the Battle of Little Big Horn happened? Would Scarlett O'Hara be knowledgeable to talk to us about her privileged life in the mansion up on Tara Hill with its wide lawns and breezy open space keeping away the *Anopheles gambiae* and *Plasmodium vivax* epidemic running amok below the hill?

But then there are other narratives by participants in their own stories who can be trusted in the first person. There's Ishmael, the only one left alive, and Holden Caulfield. Then there's Dante in his walk-ons, and Camus' Meursault who somehow manages to tell his own story after his death.

Aria reminded us that we need to concentrate on the *meaning, the meaning, the meaning,* he repeated. So we took another look at some of these details. First, the People's Liberation Army's Type 59 MBT, modeled on the Soviet T-54, the most widely mobilized tank in the world. Photographs of its intimidating presence have given prescience to looking at what happened in the square as a massacre. The death toll estimates range from a low of 241 by the Chinese government to 1,000 by Amnesty International, to a high of 10,000 by the USSR. The newly appointed American ambassador to China James Lilley tallied it in the hundreds, and the *New York Times* Pulitzer winning correspondents Cheryl WuDunn and her husband Nicholas Kristof set the number at 50 soldiers and 400-500 civilians.

A closer look at these tanks show the barrels of these turret cannons have been plugged. No division commander was to give the tank drivers the chance of making a mistake and firing an errant armor-piercing, high explosive round from the 100 mm rifled cannon into the Mausoleum of Mao Zedong where his embalmed body is a popular tourist attraction near the Gate of Heavenly Peace.

And by the time the tanks and the soldiers came into Tiananmen Square at five-thirty that Monday morning, Taiwan pop singer Hou Dejian had already negotiated safe exit routes through the square's southwest entrances for the demonstrators, leaving the square completely cleared except for the languishing pulped paper Goddess of Democracy statue.

We turned the Zoom back on and looked around at each other in silence, as if we have become portable journalists with our heads down who just copy words from digitized pixels and wait for the real writer to turn the page.

Page turner: translated from the Latin: a book so exciting or gripping that one is compelled to read it rapidly, last seen as the inconspicuous page turner in Chapter , according to our translator, slouched in his chair as if he's waiting for a fermata in

the piano's score to signal the beginning of a cadenza that is not there, at least not in this piece in which Beethoven had paid attention to the sonata form whose content did not leave room for a cadenza even when the high note of the violin held for an extra count at the end of the exposition disrupted the careful meaning of the piano's line, alarming both the pianist and the page turner as well, even though he hid it well inside the blink of an eye. His modus operandi to qualify him for this concert appointment included a cautious and imperturbable personality prepared to be the last to leave the stage in the event of a house fire, and so ordinary in dress and movement that he would not be noticed to have left the stage before the applause. He would also know the score well, as well as the pianist's preferred time for each individual page turn, especially when it's in the middle of an unusual and complicated run with a 7/8 signature.

The page turner then becomes an author, carefully placing the reader from page to page, like a mannequin whose invisible handler is shaping the words. When it's not done right, the notes from the violin and piano will collide, and the pixels on the page will decay into cosmic dust and breathe memory into another species.

When it's not done right, or the reader's placed on the wrong page, the words will be misunderstood by the translator, their idiom having lost its chromatic meaning, especially for the inattentive reader. When this happens, a clinical spectroscopy will show that the novelist, being a creation of his own imagination most of the time, will begin to feel the need to invent new musical instruments to perform his work so that it won't be encumbered by the detritus of the translator and the reader's ideas of things as they are, blue guitar or not. In other words, wrong place, wrong time, maybe a couple of centuries off.

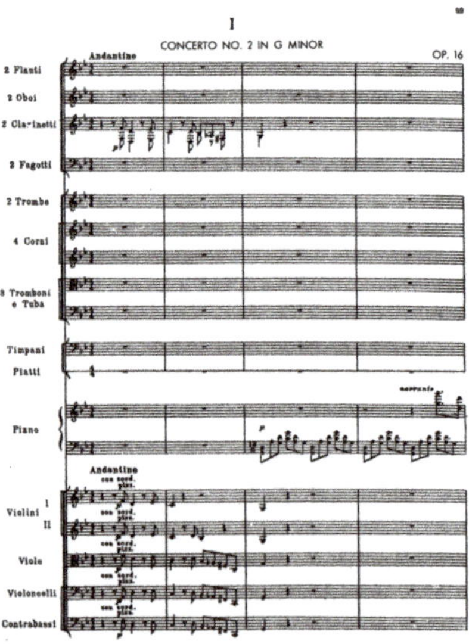

Sergei Prokofiev took a chance when he restructured and rewrote his second piano concerto ten years after the earlier copies were all destroyed in a fire. It is one of the most difficult performance pieces that all but a small handful of pianists today would avoid playing once they are old enough to experience fear and trembling.

The intensity of the crocheted runs with overlapping notes push a ferocious cadenza in double *fortissimo* to take up six minutes, half of the first movement.

The square-jawed and khaki-uniformed archivist director of the National Bibliotica of the Mind in Buenes Aires in Chapter has changed his mind and is now asking the page turner to turn the pages faster as if he were familiar with the score. He knows that the vaults in his library include a copy of the original publication of this second concerto Opus 16 in G minor that had been masked by a faked cataloging system invented by a defrocked librarian who wanted to protect it from Joseph Stalin's wrath, who held his wife and two sons hostage in a Siberian gulag in return for promises to write happy and smiling stories, even while declaring Prokofiev to be an enemy of the people, along with Shostakovich and Khachaturian.

As a dabbling pianist who gracefully accompanies the singers' merriment at family gatherings during the holidays, this archival director who had examined this unknown last remaining 1913 text that had escaped the fire and then completely rewritten from memory after ten years, he is making the final edits of an article that argues for a renumbering of this piano concerto as No. 7—after Prokofiev's incomplete No. 6 for two pianos—because it is substantially different in its content from the currently accepted No. 2, though both appear to be working the exact same form, four movements with the same markings—Andantino-Allegretto; Scherzo-Vivace; Intermezzo-Allegro moderato; Finale: Allegro tempestoso—less foursquare and slightly less precipitous in its contrapuntal fabric, a bit less imaginative in their treatment, perhaps in response to the criticism of its 1913 premier with Prokofiev as the soloist, where one reviewer claimed that cats in the tree make better music.

We now know what the cat did in the tree and why it got up there, at least according to those intentionally clueless historians, scholars and other ideologues. We may also know why Prokofiev and his tormentor Stalin both died in Moscow within one hour on the same March evening in 1953. All of Moscow's winter blooms were usurped for the leader's massive three-day state funeral, preempting any significant remembrance for Prokofiev.

In the competitive world of high level chess competition, this board game that's been around for more than fourteen centuries has acquired symbolic and political significance, like a few other mental or physical games at the international level. Chess is not just chess.

Water polo is not just water polo. The American chess prodigy Bobby Fischer's victory against a field of grand masters at Buenos Aires in the summer of 1971 brought a personal letter from President Richard Nixon: *Your victory brings you one step closer to that world title you so richly deserve, and I want you to know that together with thousands of chess players across America, I will be rooting for you when you meet Boris Spassky next year.* In 2004 Fischer renounced his U.S. citizenship.

If it's true that we are what we read and music is the allegory of our life, who we are can probably be measured and weighed by our favorite games and sports, sometimes leading to the conclusion, ***mene mene tekel upharsin***. The Russian novelist Vladimir Nabokov, under the name of Vladimir Virin, published *The Defense*, a novel without a single word of dialogue.

In a match to determine who would play the world champion, the main character Aleksandr Luzhin suffers a total mental breakdown just before the beginning of the game and totally fucks up on the first moves of his studied Luzhin Defense against his opponent's pawn-to-king-4 Ruy Lopez opening modified from the Tarrasch Defense.

He spends the rest of his life fixated on developing a chess move that would save him from losing his life, finally disappearing altogether from a high window before someone translated his novel into English, thirty-four years later. And sixty-three years after Nabokov's novel first appeared in Russian, the Italian author Paolo Maurensig published the less-noticed novel ***The Lüneburg Variation***, a modernist and suspenseful story set during the Holocaust of a double chess match between a logical and linear thinking Frisch, a German businessman, and Tabori, a Jew in one of the concentration camps who wins the return match by using an irrational sacrifice of a knight that throws the game into chaos, pushing Frisch into a panic that leads to his losing the game and to his eventual suicide, the same ending for Stefan Zweig's main character in his novella *Chess Story.*

With such focus on world class chess players and their dark side often descending into madness and suicide, it is surprising that readers of these books generally do not mind the detailed technical descriptions of the chess games but will instead forgive the authors for these trespasses. But if an author of a novel that includes the card game of bridge, on the other hand, not only will almost all readers skip the technical descriptions of the game, but they will find the author unforgiveable.

There are few novels with a bridge setting, and Alex Kuo's is one of them. In his novel *Mao's Kisses,* the main character is China's 1989 paramount leader Deng

Xiaoping's main bridge partner and personal notetaker in a story filled with detailed descriptions of the events in Beijing's political spring, as well as bridge tournaments, playing technique, and specific games. His earlier novel *shanghai.shanghai.shanghai*, included descriptions of the actual play of several deals from the 2007 Venice Cup finals held in Shanghai, including a picture of the U.S. winning team holding up an anti-George W. Bush sign made by one of the player's daughter on the back of a dinner menu at the award ceremony in response to the global criticism at their bridge table against their president, reminiscent of the John Carlos and Tommie Smith human rights salute during the 200 meters awards ceremony in Mexico City's 1968 Olympics, resulting in the prompt recall of the entire American track and field team from Mexico. The players on the women's bridge team were at first stripped of all their associations with any sanctioned game in the U.S., which included keeping them from playing professional bridge as well. (After several appeals, these draconian sentences were reduced to months of community service.)

Sports also play a defining role in how a nation sees itself. Until just a few years ago, the three-hour long baseball game had been identified as part of the American DNA. When we want to show what it means to be an American, we take a visitor to a three-hour ball game in which nothing much in the game happens for at least two of those hours, and more than that if the game has strong, dueling pitchers. Besides the major and minor professional leagues, we have the pee wee league, the little league, the Babe Ruth league, and the American Legion league. We enjoy arguing if Duke Snider or Mickey Mantle is a better player, and join Marianne Moore's wish that *Willie Mays should be a Dodger.*

Another writer with Brooklyn connections, Bernard Malamud, wrote a baseball novel *The Natural*, based loosely on the 1919 World Series scandal in which the

2 CENTS PAY NO MORE | Chicago Daily Tribune. | FINAL EDITION

BARE 'FIXED' WORLD SERIES

2 CENTS PAY NO MORE | Chicago Daily Tribune. | FINAL EDITION

CONFESSES SOX BALL PLOT

2 CENTS PAY NO MORE | Chicago Daily Tribune. | FINAL EDITION

TWO SOX CONFESS; EIGHT INDICTED; INQUIRY GOES ON

SECRECY VEILS TERMS OF U.S. SENT TO TOKIO

GRAND AND PETIT MANDATES

ALD. POWERS' HOME BOMBED; POLITICS SEEN

None Hurt; Front of House Wrecked.

Eight Fired by Comiskey; Wrecks Team

"WE THREW WORLD SERIES," CICOTTE, JACKSON, ADMIT

To Indict Gamblers Today Is Plan.

ADMIT GUILT

underpaid White Sox players conspired with gamblers and threw the series, leading to the boy's famous lament of Shoeless Joe Jackson, *Say it ain't so, Joe.*

In Malamud's novel, Roy Hobbs moves from a star pitcher to the best hitter in the history of the game, especially with his bat, *Wonderboy*, which he made from a tree split

by lightning. But the bat breaks because of Roy's misdeed—like the *Excalibur* in King Arthur's mistake—when he appeared to have accepted a bribe to throw the game, but strikes out anyway in three pitches in the final pennant game, leading a boy to cry, *Say it ain't so, Roy.*

Almost all books that feature baseball lore, real or imagined, are generally uplifting and inspiring and lead to happy endings. Even for the likeable but unlucky schmuck Roy Hobbs, and especially unusually so for Smith in Alan Sillitoe's *Loneliness of the Long Distance Runner,* quite the opposite for those doom-and-gloom novels about chess players.

American sports culture inhabited by these fans is generally very conservative: they are unctuous in their pitch for the national anthem and patriotism; wallow in aphorisms about life; wax in awe about obedience to authority; do not read more than half a book a year and obliterate the concept of the metaphor in the process of destroying the literacy of their language and its capacity to communicate anything meaningful. Even within such strictures, they also participate in sports gambling, with some ten billion dollars wagered on the college basketball championship March Madness in 2019; they ignore the sexual exploitation of coaches and widespread doping to boost performance; and they deny that sports corrupt American higher education. People like Tommie Smith, John Carlos, Colin Kaepernick and Megan Rapinoe, like the 2007 Venice Cup players, are deemed enemies of the people and often barred from participating in their sport for life. They are waiting to see whose words will survive the damage from the collision of these worlds.

By the time Aria Zoomed back into the meeting, the left half of the monitor showed the orchestral string players who had already completed their tuning standing up to welcome the vocal soloists and the guest conductor to the dais, the distinguished Otto Klemperer, for a performance of Adrian Leverkühn's oratorio, *Apocalipsis*. The Milstein sisters—violinist Maria (right) and pianist Nathali—were looking over the score of Vinteuil's violin Sonata in F♮ on the right half of the screen. And we were looking

at the parents of the composers of these two pieces, Thomas Mann in Los Angeles and Marcel Proust in Paris, the authors of *Doctor Faustus* and *Swann's Way*—who had made up the fictional Leverkühn and Vinteuil—standing behind an Aria witnessing everything they had imagined. And yes, Aria, our Aria, he finally looked bewildered in this work of imagination, maybe.

But the ever-inquisitive Milstein sisters were determined to find the real composer behind the imagined Vinteuil when the imagined sonata performed in the novel included a *little phrase* that *swept over and enveloped* the central character

Charles Swann *like a perfume or a caress.* Like grandparents reversing the ancestry search, they first went through the novel in the original French, word for word, laying out wall maps and charts and entering phrases into their laptops whenever something relating to music was mentioned, and studying the dynamics of every note of the French violin sonatas that were written during this period, trying to imagine what Proust was imagining. Finally they were convinced that he had actually heard a performance of Gabriel Pierné's Violin Sonata in D minor, Opus 36, in some salon in Paris, and which so completely captured his imagination that he remembered and passed its details on to his creation, Charles Swann. And the rest?

Leverkühn's situation is something else altogether. Aria addressed us directly. *Look,* he said, *Mann had lived in Los Angeles too long.* Imagine trying to re-invent Goethe's Faustian theme by having his composer deliberately contracting syphilis in order to inhabit a furious period of mad creativity while trying to escape the wrath of the McCarthy hearings that labeled him a communist. Who's going to perform his writing? His Schoenberg-like twelve-tone compositions were too much of a threat for the punctual Hollywood Bowl and Disneyland audience, even with the LA Philharmonic in summer residence. For them, Leverkühn and Schoenberg's work would be just noise, one way or another. However, he insisted, *this was not really a random coincidence*. In the novel, the premier of Leverkühn's *Apocalipsis* was conducted by Otto Klemperer in Frankfurt, and he was also the conductor of the LA Philharmonic between 1933 and 1939. Mann knew exactly what he was doing when he started writing this novel the year he moved into that modernist house designed for him in the Pacific Palisades suburb of Los Angeles in 1942.

We also knew then that Aria wasn't fooling around. He wanted us to be sure of that, as tenuous and enchanting as the mind and its imagination can be.

History can sometimes be terrifying, and writers trying to write about people who don't understand when their lives are shredded often outsource their work to periodic quotations from a book written by an imaginary author, or from a novel about someone who does not appear in it but who has somehow migrated into a memoir that has appeared on *The New York Times'* best-selling list that readers actually buy and talk about over and over in book clubs all over the country. Is it a novel, or is it a non-fiction, creative or not? Definitely a defying word riddle with no accompanying notes, flat or sharp.

For the subsidiary agent and inexpensive translator contracted to do the work, codes were broken without their knowledge of the target language. Just because the author's name appeared on the cover of the book didn't make it any easier. He didn't even know English. People get touristed in this book business, and the Chinese have an expression for it in the past perfect tense, ***bei lüyou.*** On a calm day without any measurable turbulence, the axial rotation of the sun guarantees that the story was factually based on something that really happened, a phenomena, and that its authenticity can be verified by the spectroscope's analysis of its luminosity even without the assistance of an author or a conductor. A reader does not have to take a cruise to distant ports to find the time to finish reading this book.

See here, he's already looking at Chapter . If we can't remember what that

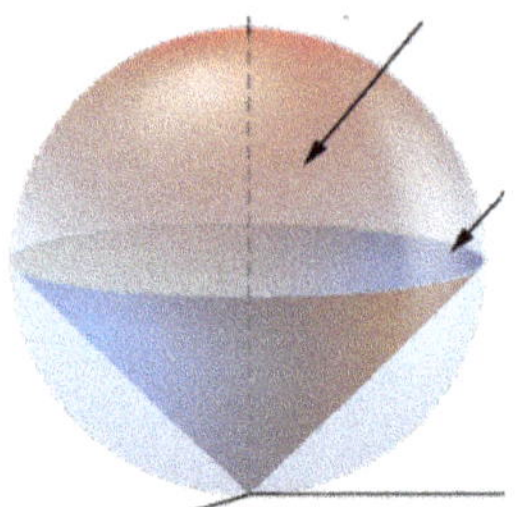

means, we can always turn to Pascal's theorem of the English alphabet for a reminder:

$x^2 + y^2 = z$. But nothing's going on with *z*. Did our author make a mistake? We're having a little geometric problem here. [EDITOR'S NOTE: What Pascal really wrote was an addition of a little superscript *2* to *z* to make it z^2 as in $x^2 + y^2 = z^2$ where for a triangle with a 90° base, the sum of its squared two sides equals the square of the diagonal hypotenuse connecting them.]

It doesn't matter that the English letter *x* is often used by writers, especially journalists, to designate material that needs further investigation or corroboration, or just as a generic substitute for missing but recognizable letters to words unacceptable to the prudent third grade teacher, or as shorthand code for a cabin of words not mentioned between writer and reader, as in Nathaniel Hawthorne's *The Scarlet Letter,* from *a* by Andy Warhol, *G* by John Berger, *S* by John Updike, *V* by Thomas Pynchon, all the way to subversive *Z* by Vassilis Vassilikos.

Alerted by these references then, perhaps they could modify our expectation that a narrative must begin with the cat going up the tree with a middle and end, or that Jack came down without a pail of water and broke his head while Jill came tumbling down and got a shredding from her mother for causing Jack's disaster. Terrifying.

In random notes explaining the characterization of the stories and their inhabitants that are gathered here, some of them are here because they were intentionally requested by the author, some conscripted as walk-ons or cameos just because they were in the neighborhood, some as proxies for uncertain identities just because they were on the nearby bookshelves, and some because they believed their work needs to be represented in this collection, whose dominion yet remains to be sorted out. In any case, they all accepted this assignment seriously, hoping that these words have meaning.

So then the balloting was serious and the result unanimous: Bach's Brandenburg Concerto No. 5 in D, BWV 1050 for flute, violin and harpsichord, with a write-in insisting it really should be renamed as his seventh or eighth keyboard concerto since both the flute and violin have only minimal solo parts compared to the keyboard's long and gigantic solo in the first movement as if Bach were inventing the cadenza for himself as a harpsichordist.

Over the last three hundred years, translators have worked within the galaxy of this cadenza first with quill and ink before moving on to music composition software with 100K memory, and with instruments that pluck, those that use pressurized air, finally settling on those that strike, before going back and trying to acquire some intellectual patent for its domain.

Having lived through the Goldberg Black Pearl Variation 25 in $B^\flat$, completed a couple of years before, into this cadenza then, these writers have waited until the second to the last chapter before walking into this novel and this Brandenburg 5 in which notes real and imagined are reproduced and repeated in so many words, to become the only ones left to tell the story.

Cadenza: Latin for improvisation, riff, a cloud of musical notes, weightless by the time of the emergency council meeting that afternoon when only six of us showed up.

We sat at one end of the long conference table trying to reconstruct the details of the book one by one, repeating them again and again, trying to be sure we had not left anything out, anything at all.

But Aria reminded us that we didn't have any evidence either—yet we believed they had occurred like before, much as we often place our trust in random coincidences and wild repetitions and in fact have come to expect them like children—and he disappeared entirely for a moment, his voice trailing into thin air.

I tried to tell everyone it'll be all right, there was no proof, no corroborating pictures to make the story credible, the republic will not panic and forget.

In a special meeting yesterday morning, the opposition printed their story, and it included specific names, dates and places for the most part as accurately as we had gathered. Aria had called just before the story first came out on twitter, then later on television. *We have been betrayed; we had all promised to be silent,* he said, *but someone has betrayed us.*

So when there was enough to fill up all the ballots in the room, Aria embraced the particulars and stood up. Believe me, it all happened so very fast no one knew for sure it wasn't an act of the imagination. *Count them,* he repeated, *count them to be sure this isn't something we'd find in tomorrow morning's papers.*

It was just as he had said, the original manuscript of this novel will be archived in the Natural Bibliotica of the Mind, he announced, along with our ballots.

INDEX

Inscription

Tsien Hsue—Shen (Qian Xuesen), Chinese, 1911-2009
Zoe Filipkowska, Polish, 1946-
Liu Cixin, Chinese, 1963-

A **•_** **1-5**

Charles Olson, American, 1910-1970
Sonny Rollins, American, 1930-
Ludwig van Beethoven, German, 1770-1827
Wolfie Mozart, Austrian, 1756-1791
Richard Wagner, German, 1813-1883
Ralph Carpenter, American, 1943-2011
Miguel del Cervantes, Spanish, 1547-1616
Alex Kuo, American, 1939-
Herman Melville, American, 1819-1891
Cao Xueqin, Chinese, 1715 (1724?)-1763 (1764?)
Wallace Stevens, American, 1879-1955
J.D.Salinger, American, 1919-2010

B **_•••** **6-9**

Ilsa Lund, Swedish, 1915-1982
Johann Sebastian Bach, German, 1685-1750
Wanda Landowska, Polish, 1879-1959
Jeremy Denk, American, 1970-
Tatiana Nikolayeva, Russian, 1924-1993
Igor Levit, Russian, 1987-
Mirjana Lewis, American, harpsichordist, 20th century
John Lewis, American, 1920-2001
Glenn Gould, Canadian, 1932-1952
Verne Edquist, Canadian, piano technician, 20th century

C _._. **10-11**

Charles Olson
John Cage, American, 1912-1992
Buckminster Fuller, American, 1895-1983
Josef Albers, German/American, 1888-1976
Anni Albers, German/American, 1899-1994
Gwendolyn Knight, American, 1913-2005
Franz Kline, American, 1910-1962
Robert Rauschenberg, American, 1925-2008
Mary Richards, American, 1916-1999
Mere Cunningham, American, 1919-2009
Albert Einstein, German, 1879-1955
William Carlos Williams, American, 1883-1963
Robert Creeley, American, 1926-2005
Robert Duncan, American, 1919-1988
Denise Levertov, American, 1923-1999
Gary Snyder, American, 1930-

D _.. **12-13**

Miguel del Cervantes

E . **14-17**

Miguel del Cervantes
Cao Xueqin
Gao E, Chinese, 1738-1815
Rush Limbaugh, American 1951-

F .._. **18-19**

Charles Olson
Herman Melville

G  _ _. **20-23**

Elizabeth I, English, 1533-1603
George Washington, American, 1732-1799
Benjamin Franklin, American, 1706-1790
Thomas Jefferson, American, 1743-1826
Minor White, American, 1908-1976
Agnes Martin, American, 1912-2004
Mark Rothko, American, 1903-1970

H  **24-25**

Beatrice Portinari, Italian, 13th century
Samuel Taylor Coleridge, British, 1772-1834

I .. **26-30**

Fritz Kreisler, Austrian, 1875-1962
Ludwig van Beethoven, German, 1770-1827
Erich Auerbach, German, 1892-1957
Witold Gombrowicz, Polish, 1904-1969
Primo Levi, Italian, 1919-1987
Susanne Langer, American, 1895-1985
René Wellek, Czech-American, 1903-1995
James Joyce, Irish, 1882-1941
Elizabeth II, British, 1926-
Joyce Kilmer, American, 1886-1918
Claribel Alegria, Nicaraguan-Salvadoran, 1924-2018
Maya Angelou, American, 1928-
Emily Dickinson, American, 1830-1886
Carolyn Forchè, American, 1950-
Joy Harjo, Mvskoke, 1951-
June Jordan, American, 1936-2002
Maxine Hong Kingston, American, 1940-

Carolyn Kizer, American, 1925-2014
Denise Levertov
Audre Lorde, American, 1934-1992
Joyce Carol Oates, American, 1938-
Adrienne Rich, American, 1929-2012

J ·_ _ _ **31-33**
Qiu Jin, Chinese, 1875-1907
Xi Jinping, Chinese, 1953-

K _·_ **34-38**
Dante Alighieri, Italian, 1265-1321
Nicholas III, Italian, 1225-1280
Brunetto Latini, Italian, 1220-1294

L ·_·· **39-41**
Ludwig van Beethoven

M  _ _ **42-46**
Albert Einstein
Mao Tse-tung, Chinese,1893-1976
Marin Mersenne, French, 17th century
Søren Kierkegaard, Danish, 1813-1855

N _· **47-50**
J.D. Salinger
George W. Bush, American, 1946-
Jiang Zemin, Chinese, 1926-
Wang Wei, Chinese, @1968-

Dick Cheney, American, 1941-
Condoleezza Rice, American, 1954-

O _ _ _ **51-53**
J.G. Ballard, British, 1930-2009

P ._ _. **54-56**
Dmitri Shostakovich, Russian, 1906-1975
James Joyce
Aram Khachaturian, Russian, 1903-1978

Q _ _._ **57-60**
Charles Olson
Gilbert Sorrentino, American, 1929-2006
Henry James, British, 1843-1916
Gertrude Stein, American, 1874-1946
Percy Lubbock, British, 1879-1915
Gyögy Lukács, Hungarian, 1885-1971
James Joyce
Franz Kafka, Czechoslovakian, 1883-1924
Saul Bellow, American, 1915-2005
John Gardner, American, 1933-1982
Agnes Martin
Cao Xueqin
Jorge Luis Borges, Argentinian, 1899- 1986
Larry McMurtry, American 1936-
Margaret Atwood, Canadian, 1939-
Dorothy Parker, American, 1893-1967
Philip Roth, American, 1933-2018
Simon Ortiz, Acoma Pueblo, 1941-

R  ._. **61-65**

Jeff Widener, American, 1956-
Mikhail Gorbachev, Russian, 1931-
Deng Xiaoping, Chinese, 1904-1997
Charlie Cole, American, AP photographer
Arthur Tsang Hin Wah, Hong Kong photographer
Stuart Franklin, British, 1956-
Wang Weilin, Chinese, 1970-
George Armstrong Custer, American, 1839-1876
Albert Camus, French, 1913-1960
James Lilley, American, 1928-2009
Cheryl WuDunn, American, 1959-
Nicholas Kristof, American, 1959-
Hou Dejian, Taiwanese, 1956-

S  ... **66-67**

Ludwig van Beethoven

T  _ **68-70**

Wallace Stevens
Sergei Prokofiev, Russian, 1891-1953
Dmitri Shostakovich
Aram Khachaturian

U  .._ **71-74**

Bobby Fischer, American, 1943-2008
Richard Nixon, American, 1913-1994
Vladimir Nabokov, Russian, 1899-1977
Paolo Maurensig, Italian, 1943-
Ruy López, Spanish, 1530-1580

Siegbert Tarrasch, German, 1862-1934
Stefan Zweig, Austrian, 1881-1942
Alex Kuo
Deng Xiaoping
John Carlos, American, 1945-
Tommie Smith, American, 1944-

V ..._ **75-77**

Duke Snider, American, 1926-2011
Mickey Mantle, American, 1931-1995
Marianne Moore, American, 1887-1972
Willie Mays, American, 1931-
Bernard Malamud, American, 1914-1986
Joe Jackson, American, 1887-1951
Alan Sillitoe, British, 1928-2010
Colin Kaepernick, American, 1987-
Megan Rapinoe, 1985-

W ._ _ **78-80**

Otto Klemperer, German, 1885-1973
Maria Milstein, French, 1985-
Nathali Milstein, French, 1995-
Marcel Proust, French, 1871-1922
Gabriel Pierné, French, 1863-1937
Joseph McCarthy, American, 1908-1957
Arnold Schoenberg, German,1874-1951

X _.._ **81-83**

Blaise Pascal, French, 1623-1662
Nathaniel Hawthorne, American, 1804-1864
Andy Warhol, American, 1928-1987

John Berger, British, 1926-2017
John Updike, American, 1932-2009
Thomas Pynchon, American, 1937-
Vassilis Vassilikos, Greek, 1934-

Y _._ _ **84-85**
Johann Sebastian Bach

Z _ _.. **86-87**

PHOTO: Zoe Filipkowska

Alex Kuo has lived most of his adult life in Idaho and Washington, with sabbaticals made possible with support from the National Endowment for the Arts, Washington State Arts Commission, Idaho Commission on the Arts, United Nations Artists Program, Rockefeller Foundation, Lingnan Foundation, and Fulbright Program.

Cadenzas is his accumulation of more than eighty years of living, listening and writing on several continents and breathing in the cadences of several languages, including three Chinese dialects.

OTHER BOOKS:

The Window Tree (poetry)
New Letters from Hiroshima (poetry)
Changing the River (poetry)
Chinese Opera (fiction)
This Fierce Geography (poetry)
Lipstick and Other Stories (fiction—American Book Award)
Panda Diaries (fiction)
White Jade and Other Stories (fiction)
A Chinaman's Chance (poetry)
The Man Who Dammed the Yangtze (fiction)
My Private China (essays)
shanghai.shanghai.shanghai (fiction)
Meeting Words at the Gate (poetry—bi-lingual)
Mao's Kisses (fiction)

redbat
books

www.ingramcontent.com/pod-product-compliance
Lightning Source LLC
LaVergne TN
LVHW052352100826
845147LV00013B/822

* 9 7 8 1 9 4 6 9 7 0 0 6 0 *

CADENZAS
a work of fiction

Alex Kuo

REDBAT
BOOKS
PACIFIC
NORTHWEST
WRITERS
SERIES

CADENZAS

a work of fiction

ALEX KUO

redbat books
2021

CADENZAS

This is a work of fiction. Names, characters, businesses, places, events and incidents are either the products of the author's imagination or used in a fictitious manner. Resemblance to actual persons, living or dead, or actual events is intentional.

Printed in the United States of America

First Edition: November 9, 2021

ISBN 978-1-946970-06-0
Library of Congress Control Number: 2021949133

Published by
redbat books
La Grande, OR 97850
www.redbatbooks.com

IMAGE CREDITS—cover: *The Goldberg Variations*, Bach (C.F. Peters); pg. 5: Charles Olsen photo by Juangris (CC BY-SA 4.0), *Cao Xueqin* by Mankong (CC BY-SA 4.0); pg. 15: *Smith Corona Silent typewriter* by P. Musgrave (CC BY-SA 3.0); pg. 19: *Tank Man Rubber Duckies* from Sina Weibo (weibo.com); pg. 21: *Tank Man* by Jeff Widener of The Associated Press; pg. 37: *Scaevola taccada-with Albatross foot prints in sand-Frigate Point Sand Island-Midway Atoll* by Foest and Kim Starr (CC BY 3.0 U.S.), *Whitetail track* by Jim Thomas (CC BY-SA 3.0); pg. 40: *Lockheed EP-3E Orion (ARIES II), USA - Navy* by Pedro Aragão (CC BY-SA 3.0); pg. 53: *Dancing bear in Bulgaria* by Bin im Garten (CC BY-SA 3.0); pg. 57: Cover of *a* by Andy Warhol (Grove Press, 1968), Cover of *Z* by Vassilis Vassilikos (edition: published by Nosso Tempo, 1975); pg. 59: Cover of T*he Defense* by Vladimir Nabakov (edition: published by Vintage, 1990); pg. 60: Cover of *Mao's Kisses* by Alex Kuo (redbat books, 2019); pg. 61: *2007 Venice Cup Winners* credit: Swan Game; pg. 62: Chicago Daily Tribune Headlines—September 23, 28-29, 1920; pg. 63; First Edition cover of *The Natural* by Bernard Malamud (Harcourt, Brace and Company, 1952), Wonderboy bat (thegoldencloset.com); pg. 66: Fritz Kreisler *Three Cadenzas*, Beethoven (C.F. Peters); pg. 67: AP Photo/Frank Augstein; pg. 71: Beethoven's First Violin Sonata (C.F. Peters/sheet music: mfiles.co.uk); pg. 73: Milstein sisters photo by Marco Borggreve; pg. 74: Cover of *Swann's Way* by Marcel Proust (Penguin Classics, Revised edition, 2004), Cover of *Doctor Faustus* by Thomas Mann (Alfred A. Knopf, 1948); pgs. 76 and 77: *Piano Concerto No. 2*, Prokofiev (Breitkoph & Hartel); pg. 79: *Ivo Pogorelich at the Metropolitan Museum of Art* Photo credit: Nan Melville for The New York Times; pg. 80: Beethoven's First Violin Sonata (C.F. Peters/sheet music: mfiles.co.uk); pgs. 81, 82, and 83: *Cello Concerto No. 1*, Shostakovich (International Music Company); pg. 85: *Brandenburg No. 5*, Bach (Barenreiter); pg. 97: *The Goldberg Variations*, Bach (C.F. Peters).

Text set in Garamond Premier Pro

Book design by
Kristin Summers, redbat design | www.redbatdesign.com

One should never write a book until he is on his deathbed, because he won't live to regret it.

—Tsien Hsue-shen, cyberneticist

Survivors are perpetrators of lies.

—Zoe Filipkowska, writer, photographer

Every era puts invisible shackles on those who have lived through it, and I can only dance in my chains.

—Liu Cixin, *The Three-Body Problem*

At first a few of them survived the classroom's filibuster and then later, the censor's bonfires. For the most part they now bunch together on our maps as hot stars, and sometimes some of them can be seen and measured with Hubble's infrared spectroscope. Depending on the precise axial rotation of the sun and making allowances for the stalking Doppler effect, a careful squint at these shrouds can be recorded to expand the spectrum of our nebulous coordinates.

When that translation happens, we call it fiction.

This is just the way this book is going to go.

As a reader, you may ask what is the origin of this book? The answer may sound absurd, and stone, cold boring. But then, we've already come this far. Let's get on with it.

Once in the village of La Mancha, there lived this spare man bordering on fifty and with indistinct features named Alonso Quijano. [PROOFREADER'S NOTE: literary scholars have disagreed on the accuracy of this name, some believing that the author had used a pseudonym to protect him.] Whatever. The meeting that evening started with a dinner of lentils and boiled mutton.

By the time of the emergency council meeting that afternoon, only five of us showed up. We idled at one end of the long conference table trying to reconstruct the notes measure by measure, repeating them again and again, trying to be sure we had not left out any word, any word at all, past all the etymology and extracts.

But Aria reminded us we didn't have any either—yet we believed these disappearances had occurred like before, much as we often place our trust in random coincidences and wild repetitions and in fact have come to expect them like children. Then he disappeared entirely, his voice trailing into thin air for the moment.

Aria had called just before the story first came out on twitter, then later on television. *We have been betrayed,* he said, *we had all promised to be silent, but someone has betrayed us.*

I tried to tell him it'll be all right, they had no proof, no corroborating evidence to make them credible, the republic will not panic.

In a special edition the next morning, the opposition printed the story anyway, and it included names of all the authors who had signed the ballots, including dates and places for the most part as truthfully as possible.

Then we did just as he had asked, signing each piece of paper folding all our promises of secrecy. There was no collusion or dissension.

So when there were enough to fill all the ballots in the room, Aria embraced the particulars and stood up. *Believe me,* he said, *it all happened so very fast no one knew for sure it wasn't an act of the imagination. Count them,* he cautioned, *count them to be sure this isn't something we'll find in tomorrow's papers.*

Who are these people who decipher and analyze the measurements of this stellar matter and transcribe them into the book that we hold in our hand while avoiding the stale debris of old truths? Here are some examples, although such random selections may only be further misleading, as anecdotes often are, like a parable or metaphor. But at this moment there is nothing else to rely on, no probability table crunched from sustainable data entries. This is all we've got for now.

In the liner notes, the author had lied and changed his name to Cervantes and moved to Madrid at the beginning of the 17th century to document something quixotically funny that no reader, editor or publisher could identify with. But no matter, its many pages would slowly appear in print, serially at first and then they kept on reappearing for hundreds of years later in one hundred and fifty languages under the title name of its main character.

Correction. Strike that. He might have changed his name to Cow a century or so later and wrote *The Story of the Stone*, even though he had never been to Beijing, or China, for that matter, and did not understand a word of its curly Mandarin, written or spoken.

The original manuscripts of these two books can now be found in the Natural Bibliotica of the Mind on Pizzumo in Buenos Aires, where Sotheby's had auctioned off some of the Third Reich's plundered treasures of paintings, sculptures, jewelry, in order to bolster their legal defense against the charges of theft and crimes against humanity. This library is open now seven days a week. During weekday mornings before noon, there, one can see the publicist, the slim archivist director, airbrushed in a photoshop parlor, square-jawed and khaki uniformed with spit-shined, brass-studded shoulder epaulets and a matching eye-scanned entry card hanging from his neck, ready to give you a tour but, please, oh please, do not touch, do not turn the pages, don't even breathe on them. And close the door behind you, please.

In addition to these manuscripts, this library had cobbled together five rogue photos in passport size of those who had attended the emergency council meeting four paragraphs back, even when the narrative text that has survived a legion of agents, censors and proofreaders mentioned six. Someone is missing. Can you guess who?

But on closer look, one of these five does not belong to the original six:

1. Who is he? Someone undercover to incite chaos, or just a writer pilfering notes down to the last detail just in case he can't remember it for his next novel?
2. Our technicians were not able to find any physical match for him, not even anything close in its colossal biometric iris scan data bank. In other words, there are two missing, with a walkin inserted just to muddy the search.
3. The author has double-counted the narrator and Aria as two separate persons, so that the accusation of betrayal would be directed to the *nom de guerre*, the imagined Aria.
4. And, just maybe, the narrator, Aria, and the author are the same person.

   Your turn. Fill in the blanks below.

Name of top left: ______________________________

Was he at the meeting? ______________________

Name of top right: ____________________________

Was he at the meeting? ______________________

Name of next left: _____________________________

Was he at the meeting? ______________________

Name of next right: ____________________________

Was he at the meeting? ______________________

Name of last: _________________________________

Was he at the meeting? ______________________

Who are the two missing? _____________________

Do you care? ________________________________

What about the author, narrator, and Aria: are they the same person? Then if not, are two of them the same person? If so, who is the one out? Each one has an equal chance of being the one out. Unless, of course, there is that fabulous chance that every one of the three is imagined. In which case, we the readers will just have to accept things as they are and not try to change them, shearsman that we're not.

Next, an examination of our nebulous coordinates.

Cadenza: Latin for improvisation, riff, a cloud of musical notes, weightless in its projective field where the line begins on the left. Or is it on the right? Like ionized gases, they vary in size from a single utterance by the recent Sonny Rollins on tenor sax, to Ludwig van Beethoven one-hundred-and-fifty years ago, whose two *cadanze* for Wolfie Mozart's piano concerto in D minor cascaded into one-hundred-and-eleven bars barely tolerant of the initial aria. From a simple sentence, to a complete chapter. And even then it ain't over until the fat lady sings, of songs no longer heard, and of books not remembered.

It's Aria again, *da capo*, return to the beginning again, a cloud of notes twittering on G, his key for most of his encrypted messages. *What happened is not an act of the imagination*, he said, and repeated it, *not an act of the imagination. Not at all*, he whispered the reiteration, as if it were a treasured secret kept from the marauding authority.

We must hide it from the censors and believers of all sorts, he cautioned, as they would surely get it wrong and misrepresent it while they ask for it to be played again or not at all in their sleepless nights in Leipzig and much later in Morocco, 1942. Then he asked each of us to swear our promise to secrecy and protect those writers whose language was competent and stable, but whose vocabulary was actually quite mundane and often ponderous in order to accurately represent the tedious rhythms and the invisible shadows of most of our lives

most of the time, where the fragility of this language attempts to combine form and content and ignore the software limits of the beginning-middle-and-end.

Who really gives a fuck how the cat got up the tree and how it got back down, our translator added.

Look at J.S. Bach's *Goldberg Variations,* he gave as an example by texting us its cover. Bach and his Nürnberg publisher had marketed it in 1741 as a keyboard exercise for instruments with two keyboards. Like a careful novelist, he used a repeated and mundane harmonic bass line by starting each note of the aria and every one of all its thirty variations with a G in the left hand, except for the last, marked a disputed *quodlibet,* appearing as the second note in the left hand, a sustained half note.

Aria ended this call with the following notation: while it appears that form and content more easily coalesce in musical compositions than in writing, especially novels, it sets up another equation when the performer is introduced, the intermediary, the translator, without whom the music does not exist, at least not to most of us. The Goldberg has been recorded more than two hundred times, from Wanda Landowska to Jeremy Denk, from Tatiana Nikolayeva to Igor Levit, Mirjana and John Lewis, and then there is of course that eccentric pianist from Toronto, Glenn Gould on his Steinway CD318, and his nearly blind tuner Verne Edquist.

That left us with another question: has the performer then become the form, and the music score the content, or the other way around? Or has that question only become an ordinal issue for the attentive listener or the discerning reader?

The marked time signature in a musical score can change dramatically to the experienced ear that faults the hubris of time as determined chronologically by the beginning, middle, or end, especially in a narrative such as a novel. Within the nebula of multi-dimensional string theory, time in its four dimensional nebulum becomes relative, in the process gaining additional properties that include the Möbius revolutionary cycle in which a moment in time can be overlapped and repeated time and again, utterly

$$\chi\ (u,v) = (1 + \tfrac{v}{2} \cos \tfrac{u}{2}) \cos v$$

$$y(u,v) = (1 + \tfrac{v}{2} \sin \tfrac{u}{2}) \sin u$$

$$z(u,v) = \tfrac{v}{2} \sin \tfrac{u}{2}$$

destroying the concept of beginning, middle and end, making it possible to have a memory of the future inhabiting a moment of an imagined past. Within that configuration of time, then, did the cat ever go up the tree? Or, if it did, did it ever come down? Or did the cat start by being up in the tree in the first place?

Such deliberate examination of the scale of our language takes for granted that words matter. Just maybe no word is that transparent or important in all of its chromatic fantasies.

Where the line begins on the left is another matter altogether. Breaking the hierarchical chains of traditional education, in 1933 a group of American educators opened a collective school in North Carolina and named it Black Mountain College. Emphasizing an interdisciplinary and experimental approach with emphasis on the arts, the college did not hold formal classes, and became a precursor to such schools as UC at Santa Cruz in California, Marlboro in Vermont, Shimer in Illinois, Roger Williams in Rhode Island, and Evergreen in Washington. It eliminated all curricular requirements and grades, dismissed classes, and everyone in residence was expected to participate in cultivating the campus, from tilling the farm to peeling the potatoes in the kitchen.

In the transformative and creative space the college provided before it ran out of gas in its short longevity of twenty-four years, it gathered such radical residents as John Cage and Buckminster Fuller, Josef and Anni Albers, Gwendolyn Knight and Franz Kline, the deKoonings and Robert Rauschenberg, Mary Richards and Merce Cunningham, and its visiting lecturers included Albert Einstein and William Carlos Williams.

And there were no lines on campus, that is, not until the poet and essayist Charles Olson came along as the rector of the college in 1956 and started talking trash about the philosophy of writing poetry, and then publishing it, as if everyone was paying attention, uh-huh. There he is, in that portrait

of him in Chapter  with his chin resting on his left hand, caught in a rare moment with his mouth shut before ordering the line for questions to form to his left. Or was it to his right?

In what his supporters claim as the manifesto for the Black Mountain poets movement—whatever a movement is—he introduced the topic of *projective verse*, essentially proclaiming how organic poetry should be written to get away from the debilitating shrines of conventional and academic poetry. To be free, poetry must be written in an open field in which it goes from the head to the ear and then to the syllable, and from the heart to the breath and then to the line. And above all, the length of each line should be determined by the breath of the poet rather than a conventionally predetermined meter, he added, later crystallized by Robert Creeley: *form is never more than an extension of content.*

The American poets who accepted his invitation to join this mixed-media collage included Robert Creeley, Robert Duncan, Denise Levertov, and Gary Snyder, and the group became identified as the Black Mountain Poets, until Olson himself exposed it: this *whole* Black Mountain Poet *thing is a lot of bullshit*, in a National Poetry Myth month when he was accused of white male imperialism and misogyny.

Just maybe artists should refrain from talking and writing about their work, be they dancers, pianists, painters or writers. It can only get them into more trouble.

Since he had no desire to remember the name of the village that was home to the character he made up named Alonso Quijano, the closest the sixteenth/seventeenth century Spanish author Miguel de Cervantes came to identifying it was the agricultural La Mancha region around the coordinates of 30° North and 4° West. A spare man with gaunt features and a great sportsman, he stayed up nights reading romances until they addled his mind and, like a viral contagion, infected his soul as well. He abandoned his silk doublets, velvet breeches and shoes to match for the holidays and dedicated the rest of his life to the role of a knight-on-an-errand, restoring chivalry and easily slipping into the heroic madness of saving himself and his country.

Actually, it's madness what writers will go through to make up the personalities of their characters in their pages of fiction. A little remembered detail from here and there, something read or seen in a movie, sometimes something entirely made up, something borrowed, something stolen, something broiled medium rare.

And so here it comes.

The first thing Cervantes had to do was change the name of Alonso Quijano to the more distinguished Don Quixote de la Mancha. Next, Don Quixote had to have a terrific young horse with a reliable name that didn't eat too much and obeyed commands, which DQ renamed Rocinante. Then of course he had to find someone smart enough to attend to all his needs, including keeping his lance in shape. With the promise of giving him a governorship, he found a farm hand with another made-up name, Sancho Panza, and mounted him on a sturdy donkey named Dapple for their journey.

The challenges of separating reality and its representation circulate throughout this early novel, not only for Cervantes writing the narrative, but for the characters themselves. The stories Don Quixote and Sancha Panza hear on their journey become their stories, and they become agents and writers participating in reshaping their own cameo histories. At certain crucial points in this episodic novel whose different scenes can be shuffled into any order, the reader is tempted to join the horse and donkey parade searching for their author.

No, Cervantes did not change his name to Cow, but another writer with a similar sounding name did, Cao Xueqin, who lived near Beijing a century later, though he was born 200 leagues away in Nanjing. And actually, living in eighteenth century China, he was conversant in both the northern plains Beijing Mandarin curly dialect, as well as Nanjing's southern harsher and less-rounded version. He spent a decade writing *The Story of the Stone* in vernacular Chinese, with the manuscript in some eighty chapters unfinished on his sudden death in 1763 and, with an additional forty chapters from notes and edited by his painter friend Gao E, it was not published until thirty years later.

Which could happen to writers back then who lived in Beijing and drank too much cheap rice wine, or now to those who are shackled when they disturb the State Administration of Press and Publication's watchful censors.

Located in an enormous mansion in an imagined Beijing, this novel describes in excruciating detail the social and financial interaction and tension of an extended family and their servants, in the process revealing their privileged daily lives in the trifling and manicured but strict hierarchy of manners in which a wrongly-placed pair of chopsticks or a careless utterance would have dire consequences. With a cast of hundreds, they whiled away their hedonistic lives in sumptuous dinners and lavish parties, trading domestic gossip, listening to some melody on a qin or pipa, playing complicated board games,

and participating in the poetry club that was scheduled to meet weekly.

With some encouragement and funding from the family elders, the poetry club decided to invite an internationally renowned commentator to be the judge of the season's finale of its highly competitive poetry workshop sessions just before the Autumn Moon celebrations. They decided to ask the American Rush Limbaugh, the recent recipient of the Presidential Medal of Freedom, who readily accepted and had in fact begun taking notes of this event for his next book. As a safety precaution, the club also invited the correspondent and writer of this work of fiction, Alex Kuo, and helped him get through the tight customs inspection for his Smith Corona Silent typewriter

which he needed to record everything said or unsaid as truthfully as possible.

Oddly enough, Limbaugh had no trouble with customs when he stepped off his PanAm Sikorsky Flying Boat flight from San Francisco with a duffle bag filled with repackaged Chinese firecrackers that he had planned to resell in China at

a jacked up price in order to balance the trade deficit between the two nations.

The dozen finalists were fully prepared for this contest, with the moderator introducing the honorable Mr. Limbaugh, and the correspondent sitting in the back with his Silent typewriter. The poets had their own desks, with identical brush and paper, and ink of the same density prepared equally and distributed by the servants so they would not have to do it. Some of them looked quite young, still in their teens. But the correspondent could tell from their confident postures that from their ten years of intense tutoring in the classics they could recite from rote even the most obscure classical poem on demand and not miss a word.

The instructions were clear, a competition in couplets in sequence, with no restraints on metrics or rhymes. The moderator will begin with a line, and based on a random drawing, the first competitor will add another line to form a couplet before writing a third line which will become the first line of the next competitor's couplet. The only requirements demanded the inclusion of a profound metaphor and reciting the completed lines to the gathering.

Mr. Limbaugh supplied,

> *Last night the north wind blew the whole night through*

To which the first competitor added

> *Today outside my door the snow still flies*

to complete the couplet before composing another line to form the first line of the couplet for the next competitor.

> *On mud and dirt its pure white flakes fall down*

In the back our correspondent could hear someone whisper a snivel about these lines: *No good, no good; I can't under-*

stand a word of it, and he typed it into his typewriter, using the red ribbon for every word of it .

And powered jade the whole earth beautifies
Flakes on the dead plants weave a winter dress

Another said, *That sounds like something written by a trained parrot.*

And on dry grasses gemlike crystalize
Now will the farmer's brew a good price fetch

She's the worst poet in the group, every time the worst. I don't know how she ever made it to the finals.

His full barn to a good year testifies
The ash-filled gauge shows winter's solstice near

Yeah, that metaphor is so profound it'll be sure to confound the reader.

And the frost the river's motion petrifies
Snow settles thickly on sparse willow's boughs

Yucko, she needs more potty training.

In snowbound woods a bough's creek terrifies
The wind-blown snow around the traveler whirls

This is going to be the moment of her life. Pity, pity.

An hour later, the visiting expert Mr. Limbaugh selected these winning lines,

Which, behold in beauty, winter's blasts despise
The hushed yard startles to a cold chough's chatter

before stuffing the cash honorarium into his pocket and rushing to the airport toting his duffle bag filled with the most expensive *Maotai* he could find at the Friendship Store in downtown Beijing.

Sounding annoyed and a bit distracted, Aria called and said we must release a statement to sustain the readers' confidence in this novel, this work of fiction. We have to come up with someone they can trust, he emphasized, some witness with a reliable memory to make this story that we inhabit compelling and convincing and worthwhile, at least for the moment. We are facing the international media deluge of varying and sometimes conflicting versions of what actually happened in Beijing's political spring of 1989, each with its own self-serving agenda, each one surrounded by a mirage of details, including videos and interviews. How can facts have meaning, in whatever form, he asked in desperation. Our work depends on our looking carefully at the content of these facts, what they mean.

So we bent over and carefully scribbled down our nominations on the little squares of paper handed out by the prefect, who collected them, tallied the totals, and announced the popularity: the Tank Man.

This photoshopped image is heisted from one of the three shots taken by Jeff Widener, who like the other 1,200 journalists and photographers, was assigned to Beijing to cover the historic meeting between Mikhail Gorbachev of the USSR and Deng Xiaoping to mend the Sino-Soviet relationship. [EDITOR'S FACTUAL NOTES: similar photographs were taken that Monday morning, June 5, by Charlie Cole of *Newsweek*, Arthur Wah of Reuters, Stuart Franklin of Magnum, from Beijing Hotel's sixth floor balconies facing west toward Tiananmen Square, over the red hair of a giant Ronnie McDonald in lotus position on the same street, East Chang'an Avenue. Widener of the Associated Press took his photographs–on borrowed film from an exchange student—with a Nikon FE2 camera and a 400 mm lens in Fuji 100 color negative film. Among many awards, this photograph was a finalist for a Pulitzer.]

Surely our readers would think this Tank Man with *Time* magazine's accolade as one of the 100 most important people of the 20th century would be someone whose active witness account would make him a reliable narrator.

[MORE EDITOR'S FACTUAL NOTES OF FACT: There are videos of him facing a column of Type 59 main battle tanks

from the 1st Armored Division of the 65th Group Army. These tanks were made in Factory 617 in Mongolia owned by Norinco, short for China North Industries Group Corporation Limited, one of the world's largest military contractors.]

Some rumors have identified him as a nineteen-year old student named Wang Weilin who was charged with political hooliganism, but Chinese officials speaking anonymously, said that their data base was flummoxed by this claim. One of President Richard Nixon's deputy special assistants with the support of PEN International and Hong Kong's Center for Human Rights, made a speech to the President's Club in which he alleged that the Unknown Rebel was executed two weeks later, denied by Politburo member Jiang Zemin, who said *I think never killed*. There have also been reports that this Wang Weilin [sic] was a Peking University graduate student who had too much to drink after his dissertation defense had to be postponed because of the student demonstrations on campus and just before he was to leave for Taiwan and become a taxidermist at the National Palace Museum. And another that said he was an undercover tank commander trying to realign the tank column to minimize the damage to the old cobbled sections of Tiananmen Square.

Are eyewitness accounts reliable, we asked. Rhetorically, would Lieutenant Colonel George Armstrong Custer be a good source for why the Battle of Little Big Horn happened? Would Scarlett O'Hara be knowledgeable to talk to us about her privileged life in the mansion up on Tara hill with its wide lawns and breezy open space keeping away the *Anopheles gambiae* and *Plasmodium vivax* epidemic running amok below the hill?

But then there are other narratives by participants in their own stories who can be trusted in the first person. There's Ishmael, the only one left alive, and Holden Caulfield. Then there's Dante in his walk-ons, and Camus' Meursault who somehow manages to tell his own story after his death.

Aria reminded us that we need to concentrate on the *meaning, the meaning, the meaning*, he repeated. So we took another look at some of these details. First, the People's Liberation Army's Type 59 MBT, modeled on the Soviet T-54, the most widely mobilized tank in the world. Photographs of its intimidating presence have given prescience to looking at what happened in the square as a massacre. The death toll estimates range from a low of 241 by the Chinese government to 1,000 by Amnesty International, to a high of 10,000 by the USSR. The newly appointed American ambassador to China James Lilley tallied it in the hundreds, and the *New York Times* Pulitzer winning correspondents Cheryl WuDunn and her husband Nicholas Kristof set the number at 50 soldiers and 400-500 civilians.

A closer look at these tanks show the barrels of these turret cannons have been plugged. No division commander was to give the tank drivers the chance of making a mistake and firing an errant armor-piercing, high explosive round from the 100 mm rifled cannon into the Mausoleum of Mao Zedong where his embalmed body is a popular tourist attraction near the Gate of Heavenly Peace.

And by the time the tanks and the soldiers came into Tiananmen Square at five-thirty that Monday morning, Taiwan pop singer Hou Dejian had negotiated safe exit routes for the demonstrators, through the square's southwest entrances, leaving the square completely cleared except for the languishing pulped paper Goddess of Democracy statue.

We turned the Zoom back on and looked around at each other in silence, as if we have become portable journalists with our heads down who just copy words from digitized pixels and wait for the real writer to turn the page.

Aria had cautioned us to be sure it'll not be found in tomorrow's papers, but he was wrong. It did, on August 6 and August 9 anyway, right after the world's first use of WMD that led to the end of World War II and captured by every major newsreel broadcasting company in the world, including Pathé and Movietone News. With that early disclosure which would seem to have erased the necessity of caution, the author of this work of fiction then decided to make a cameo appearance here and address the reader in the third person. As a six-year old he was living in Shanghai's French Concession on those

dates and could have seen the flash of the plutonium 240 implosion at eleven miles high over Nagasaki 500 miles away, even at eleven in the morning, at least according to J.G. Ballard's Jim Graham, who saw it as *an unbroken silence lay over the surrounding land, as if the sun had blinked, losing heart for a few seconds.*

For Kuo, then, he had to wait fifty-three years to find the language and will to describe what it was like for him, a poem under the title of "The Day the War Ended."

I was six the day the war ended in 1945
But I don't remember which flag I waved

There were carnivals everywhere
The regulators were beginning to disappear

The radio station sent out free news
Prison doors opened for fifty today, one hundred tomorrow

One by one they came out, the Red Cross relocating
The head in one place, the feet in another

Most said nothing, others still stood in line
Promising to vote "A" or "A" in the next election

There I am, in that photograph trying to look away
The day the war ended on this street corner

Those others gathered around me were waiting
Blowing out kisses to Movietone News

They lingered, trying to believe whatever happened
That day will not be repeated in anyone's history

Now at more than a half century since that war ended
Our stories are still hedged between hurt and hope

Most of the time I'm watching eyewitness news
As if I'm seeing something taking place in the past

Or between there and here whatever the time
These intolerances have not stopped, whatever the place

This is what it was like exactly that day after
With nothing left to be taken away

Someone is tracing a distant coincidence
Another is doing the same in his head

No one is waiting for messages or decisions
Our fists gripped in ambiguity, between wars

Into the conventional cadenza in which notes real and imagined are reproduced, writers real and imagined walk into this work of fiction which you are holding. It is Charles Olson's turn to make a cameo for the third time for no reason other than Grove Press publishing his *Call me Ishmael* in 1947. Olson had not made up that title, but Herman Melville used it nearly a century ago as the first line in the third chapter of his one hundred and thirty-five chapter whaling novel *Moby-Dick.* Melville had left most of the story-telling to Ishmael in the first person narrative, except where he walked into the story to provide the necessary backgrounding unavailable to Ishmael, such as in the novel's first two chapters' prequel in which a grammar school teacher and a librarian's assistant laboriously presented a rough history of whaling in the mid-nineteenth century, during which 735 of the global 900 whaling vessels were owned by New Englanders and sailed out of Nantucket, Maine, a whopping 80 percent.

Two thirds of this terraqueous globe are the Nantucketer's, said the omniscient Melville intruding into Chapter 14.

Next, he added, *For the sea is his; he owns it, as Emperors own empires.*

And next, the composer of this cadenza dips my best nib into the inkwell and rewrites the title of Melville's novel:

Moby-Dick: The Hunt of a Lifetime

And, furthermore, convinced that Melville believed that the wish to overwhelm nature lies at the bottom of our hearts,

he made up an inscription in quatrains to begin the novel, and repeated it at the end, as if Ishmael had written it twice.

I am a hunt of a lifetime volunteer
Making dreams come true
I am not paid in money, though I have a sponsor
Safari International
I seek not fame or glory, but I am thankful
To be part of the story, I try to make a difference
For we all know what's in store
To light up America and more

At last then, the two hundred ton *Pequod*—with three new masts and embellished with whale body parts, including its captain Ahab's prosthetic leg and its tiller carved from a sperm whale's jawbone—was picked out from Nantucket's Straight Wharf, provisioned for three years, and readied with a fresh crew to set sail for the Pacific by way of the South Atlantic and the Cape of Good Hope on its hunt of a lifetime. Its mission was to return with its hold filled with sperm whale oil for its Quaker owners' ledger, but by now just about anyone who has read an American novel, even in translation, must know that it was actually its captain's revenge voyage for a whale that took his leg, ending in sinking the *Pequod* and killing everyone except the one left to tell the story in his attempt to square the circle.

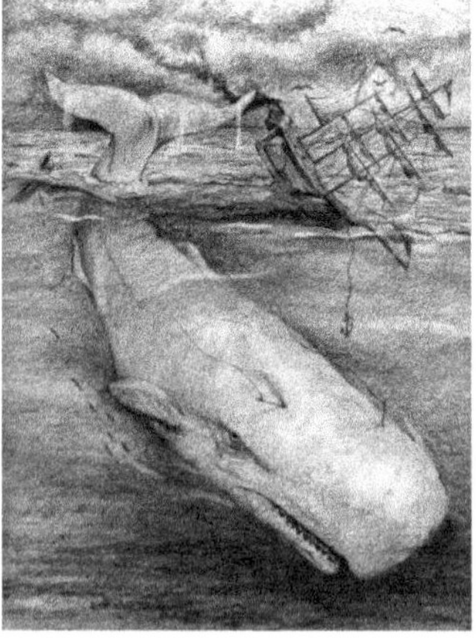

The thing is, often writers are so fixated on the historical accuracy of their work that they leave out the truth. Most of the time there isn't a choice, but once in a while there is. Dante had to make some choices in his *Divine Comedy* seven hundred years ago. Pope Nicholas III kept his name in the Eighth Circle of Hell, and Dante's teacher Brunetto Latini kept his in the Seventh Circle, while the woman he admired kept hers as she wandered around freely in *Paradiso*, as did Dante as a walkin throughout the long poem.

We have come to expect alternate realities as real things, even though we do not have any evidence to make them credible. Like that time when the hunting guide got out of his pickup at the Trailways depot, still thinking about what an anonymous Tehran woman had said in an interview for a magazine piece he read earlier that morning: *I have come to regard men and violence as inseparable.* He thought about the wolf and how its body had been torn apart bone by bone, from the *metatarsal* to the *sesamoid* to the *tarsal* hanging on the barbed wire fence in every township and range in the American west. From the *Canis lupus* to the elk now, wapiti, *Cervus canadensis,* its head mounted and hanging in restaurants at truckstops on Interstates 70, 80, and 90 all the way west to the Pacific Ocean from the Mississippi River. Then bang, a door slammed shut next to him, and everything simply evaporated, bones and all.

An obese woman had shut the door at the bus terminal, and stood next to him now starting to wave a hand at the first

passenger stepping off the bus, a troll of bracelets gnarling down her raised flabby arm, a cigarette in the other. The three of them looked at each other, standing there on the same piece of pavement between Interstates 80 and 90, 300 miles from the Pacific. Must be her son, looking like a pvt in civvies returning from basic, barely old enough to have graduated from high school, a young boy stuffed into the body of a man with baseball hat. And this didn't just happen anywhere, not in Madrid, Buenos Aires, Casablanca, Black Mountain, Warsaw, Beijing or Nantucket, but right there in downtown Lewiston, Idaho.

The next to step down was the young guest from Freedom, Pennsylvania, but he looked much older after months of chemotherapy for terminal Hodgkin's. Hair cut short to the stubble like the pvt's, loose in Cabela's overstock of desert camos in tank top, pants, boots, and watch-strap, dressed for his Hunt of a Lifetime. The guide walked up to the boy and tugged on his matching camoed rifle case and duffel bag and called him, *John*?

The boy was speechless, finally asking, *you're my hunting guide, what? You're my hunting guide? Funny name, G. G stands for what?*

G was patient, this kid's got only a few months left to live, for chrissakes. Yes, me heathen Chinee no play poker here in Idaho six generations, name means double trouble or dragon eater, whatever.

John wanted to see the town a little the next morning, starting at the airport where he identified the mounted Lockheed F-80 Shooting Star, yes, right, a Korean War veteran clouded in silver and returned from the Peruvian Air Force in a lend-lease reversal and gifted to Lewiston.

And what do they do around here, John pointed to a couple of men handing out free red bibles outside a high school.

They go to karaoke bars, rodeos and monster truck rallies. Be nice G, be nice. They trash evolution and climate change,

good country people unburdened by humility or mercy. And they watch football and they hunt and kill everything.

It's pretty much the same in Freedom, John said, just thirty minutes from the Pirates, Penguins, and Steelers, and the foundation that grants hunting adventures to children with terminal illnesses. *But it'll make my dream come true,* furrows gathering on his forehead and trying to forget the sickness in his lungs and liver and the months of radiation that seared his hair and took away his flesh.

At the entrance to the city park a reader board offered free pizza and a pitcher of beer to successful hunters who've shot a wolf in the open season that started with the Lewis and Clark expedition two centuries ago, the ongoing blood lust annexed to state law just a year ago.

The sunrise was well over an hour away when they came to the end of the dirt road at Little Boulder Creek and parked next to a camper, its back window filled with NRA, Marines and POW-MIA stickers. G flashed the light to the dry creek bed that'll take them most of the way up to the lookout point, about thirty minutes or so, *not too close right behind me, sling your rifle with empty chamber,* the light from his headlamp bouncing as he brushed aside fall's spider webs stretched across

the trail, turning around and checking just to be sure John was right with him, hand swatting the light on his face.

They were near the top when the reflection of the glowing sunrise behind McGary Butte silhouetted the saddle along the ridge line where they took a rest and waited until it was light enough to believe what they were seeing in the emerging landscape. Boxed lines here to demark the boundary of a BNSF clearcut, a color there separating ponderosas from white firs, and the distant shadows slipping over the slope down to the Clearwater in the next township and range. G imagined he could taste the tang of the season's last golden asters above the dust.

It's here, John whispered and handed the binoculars. *I like him; I like his rack; I like his size and the way he moves.*

It's still a quarter-mile away; we have to get closer.

But John was ready. He had waited months for this moment to kill something. His bolt locked a shell into the chamber of his .308, moving through dew-covered sage, the elk continuing to graze upwind, oblivious and comfortable in its own domain in the warmth of the gathering sunlight, a set of six-point antlers showing when they were 200 yards out. Prone, John peered into his scope until the black dot centered on the elk at a point up from the front leg and just back of the shoulder for a lung and heart shot in this perfect hunt he had dreamed about and practiced for in which he carried his own rifle, squeezed the trigger and did his own killing, and wham, the Winchester 180 grain Black Talon hollow point bullet twisting out of the 24-inch barrel and into the target at more than 2,000 foot-pounds, its recoil slamming back into his shoulder.

G waited a moment before he ran to the downed elk with its forelegs twitching and chest still heaving, and to end the searing pain ripping into the bull's lungs and flesh, he quickly snapped the safety off his own rifle and fired a shot straight

into the elk's head just behind the occipital bone facing him, killing him instantly, first for the elk, then for the boy, then for the rest of us, dead or alive, wanted or not.

Next, a picture was taken of the kneeling John for his keepsakes. Another for the foundation. A third for the *Lewiston Tribune.*

The next day G helped John with the duffle and rifle case at the bus depot. Hunt of a Lifetime paid a local taxidermist to shoulder-mount the elk head and picked up the shipping charges to Pennsylvania for the 200 pounds of custom cut-and-dry-iced flesh connected to it. John left town still a young boy who had just made his choice to take a life, just as his own would be taken from him before Christmas without his choice.

The western history of the nebulous coordinates must queue from QE I, the Good Queen Bess who ruled over England for almost the entire second half of the sixteenth century, a good hundred years before it gifted its Red Cross to the Union Jack. Under the strict parameters of a steady room temperature and comfortable humidity, Her Highness established legal standards by ordering the construction of physical models for the measurement of volume, weight and distance.

A little more than one hundred and fifty years later, the same process was duplicated in the United States with the support of Washington, Franklin and Jefferson, just before the nation opened up the greatest land sale in history. *Yankee Doodle went to town a-riding on a pony.*

In order to establish some order and structure to this huge land grab at the end of the nation's Civil War, Congress passed a bill in 1785 authorizing the General Land Office in the Treasury (later as the U.S. Geological Survey within the Department of the Interior) to survey and inventory the nation's public lands so their designated units could be identified, sold, stolen or given away. *Stuck a feather in his cap and called it macaroni.*

The principle methodology mapped the nation's public lands by using measurement units based on the distance of a mile legalized by QE I as 5,280 feet and squared to form a Section of one squared mile of six hundred and forty acres (an acre is based on the English measurements of *rods* and

surveyor's chains or more accurately, the size of a plat of arable land that can be tilled by one farmer behind one oxen in one day with a thirty minute lunch break) and located within a Township and Range of thirty-six similar Sections numbered horizontally consecutively from right to left and offset against a baseline of North Pole to South Pole principal meridians.

The photographer Minor White once told some students at the La Grande Arts Center in Oregon some eighty years ago that it's the eye that sees the picture, not the camera. He also discouraged the proliferation of the repetitious pretty picture, and thought it should have been left in the acid bath because it did not add anything to our visual landscape.

A few years later one of his students teaching photography at the University of Idaho had come to believe that the mind behind this eye is often filled with linguistic abstractions, a contagious vocabulary of words. The very names of these life forms control what we see and how we see them, like fingers pointing. Sometimes we can't even see it unless we have a lexicon and dictionary to index and explain its existence, often mimicking its symbol and preventing us from experiencing what it really is.

He thought that the most common issue raised by those resistant viewers of abstract paintings such as those by Agnes Martin or Mark Rothko, is coded in their question "But what is it?" What they want is a name or title for the painting, such as *Vase of Tulips*, or *Sunset*, something they can literally relate to. These words do not however exist in total isolation: they are laced with a configuration of inchoate visual fragments, a random pictorial remembrance of images from our imagined past. Together, they form a visual barrier to what the artist actually sees in our natural environment.

One early fall morning he took his equipment down to the Snake River south of the Hells Canyon Dam, on the Idaho

side. He wanted to do some representational work with his most reliable 50-mm lens to minimize the lies, and without the blue guitar.

Stepping through a field of Columbia River basalts, volcanic rocks, and billeted metamorphosed ancient ocean floor, along the suture zone between older North America and all of the western United States accreted over 100 million years ago, he took a mental inventory of their composited habitations: pictographs, petroglyphs, mine entrances, inadvertent and deliberate destruction of plants and land forms from hunting, fishing, and camping, evidence of human and horse traffic, as well as water erosion created by the wakes from the excursion and power boats, and, from an old Chinese miners' camp, a Del Monte sardine can dated from the 1930s, during the Great Depression.

Into the second hour of his traverse over this scrum, he noticed an unusual brighter color of sedimentation of hydrated uranium oxides on a large piece of metamorphic rock. He loaded a roll of Agfa Ultra print film into his Nikon F5 and screwed it onto a tripod, focused the lens, and waited a good two hours until the light was just right before pressing the shutter, just once.

For his notebook he copied down the coordinates from his cell phone as 45.635° North and 116.484° West, and from the USFS map in his kitbag he located this rock at the northeast corner of the northwest corner of Section 20, Township 2 North, and Range 51 East.

Back at the parking lot he was greeted by two teenagers in camo yelling and grinning next to their pickup truck with Idaho 1L plates while they loaded their rifles in matching camo, getting ready for their big hunt. Their school had been cancelled to observe the first day of deer season.

Yanker, didel, doodle down, diddle, dudel, lanther, Yanke viver, voover vown, Botermilk und *tanther.*

There it is, faithfully located in fifthteenth century Holland before it was translated into English and adopted as Connecticut's state song five centuries later in the middle of deer season, along with all the buttermilk one could drink.

Believe me, the parched mariner said, and held us with his glittering eye and skinny hand. It all happened so very fast no one knew for sure it wasn't an act of the imagination, he continued. And I was the only one who lived to tell the story; we stood still and listened as three-year-olds. Actually, he said, actually I'm the only one who didn't die, actually creating for us the world of wonderment inhabited by both the not-living and the dead that challenged Beatrice in both *Paradiso* and *Purgatorio*.

We now know that shooting an albatross with a bow isn't exactly the same as

shooting a whitetail deer with a rifle—even though they both end in sadness—but not to the painful depth of our storyteller whose exculpation demanded his periodic confession of his doomed voyage to the South Pole, encountering horrendous

winds and waves that make the winter passage through the Bay of Biscay the red sky of a sailor's delight, the ***Die Glückliche Zeit*** of German submarine wolfpacks attacking the Allied merchant shipping lanes in 1940-42 and successfully sinking nearly nine hundred vessels with five million tons of war materiel.

But by early 1943, the team of military strategists and search theorists came back with what they had been asked to do. Each file they submitted unfolded a series of actionable directives to locate those twelve hundred diesel-powered U-boats that had to cross somewhere in that 130,000 square miles of the Bay on their way to the Allied shipping lanes in the Atlantic, embarking from or returning to their home ports on the west coast of France.

First, bomb these home ports.

Second, since these submarines could not transit submerged for the distance of the Bay, use aircraft to look for the surface wake they leave behind even at periscope depth with decks awash. Train the navigators in the American Lockheed Martin B-24 and PBY Catalina to stick to the five basic search patterns that were developed using the record of previous sightings as a baseline, especially in moments of repetition and boredom. Use them, especially the Square and the Barrier, but allowing some degree of randomness, as some of these German skippers often challenged the rigid hierarchy of their command planners.

And third, above all, audit the German Enigma naval communications, since the code had already been cracked by those Polish mathematicians months before the Luftwaffe's Junkers and Heinkels leveled most of Warsaw. Here, no non-disclosure compact was signed, no promise was made to keep it a secret: no collusion or dissention. He did live to tell the story, again and again.

The music score was never entirely blank, but splattered with spilled ink and a mélange of notes as if we know the history of how and when each of them came into our life and has since acquired a familiarity that challenges our memory. The same for the canvas that was never white to begin with, its flecks of drying latex paint, never plain white to begin with, or the paper loaded into our printer just waiting for the blank white space on the computer in the next room to be filled with enough tiny black pixels to form two-hundred-and-fifty words so that the document could be Wi-Fied to the waiting printer.

For Jerome David Salinger, he started at this beginning then, with the same white pages in his manual typewriter in front of him. But this is hardly an empty space, a space in which the shapes and the writer's intent are constantly changing. Bouquets of parentheses started hurdling out of his notebook, raising high his expectation that the leftover Buddy from a previous story would now take over and try to understand and tell the story of his brother Seymour to unknown readers, pulling imagined snapshots out of his wallet to help him.

And as luck would have it, this Buddy decides that he wants his own story and just ups and walks away with J.D. chasing after him, notebook in hand, each detail stumbling into the next one word at a time until they reach an irreparable and delicate balance.

Into Buddy's story then, we see him as one of the twenty-three in the flight crew on an aerial electronic surveillance flight seventy-miles from China's Hainan Island's Lingshui Naval Base in an Aries II on its return flight to Kadena Air Base in Japan. With a quarter tank of unspent fuel, the pilot had decided to loiter a few more moments trying to suck up any electronic debris to pass off to fleet command as well as submarines in

the vicinity, just long enough to provoke a pair of Chinese J-8 Finback interceptors to

play a cat-and-mouse game with the ferret intruder. The young top gun Finback pilot came in too fast on its second pass at Mach 2 and sheared the Aries II port wing, the shattering sound reverberating backward through the aircraft's entire frame, trashing its number one engine before it spun out of control into a doomed vortex toward the ocean 25,000 feet below.

The Aries pilot had already sent out the Mayday PB-20N Kilo Romeo 919 70 nautical miles SSE of Hainan Island collision with Finback 070 at 22,500 Mayday signal, and the crew followed immediately, declined every number down to zero on every keyboard, slammed the dedicated F12 key three times, manually destroyed the drives on the five laptops on board, and dumped all the operational binders already printed on acetate-treated paper that will dissolve in water into crypto boxes that were shoved out the starboard hatch, before a double check and EDP completed, sir.

The PLA allowed the Aries to make an emergency landing at Lingshui and the crew of the spy plane to stay for the next ten days in the air conditioned military hotel before they were flown out on a Continental Boeing 737 after each crew member was charged $34 for an exit visa out of China, probably forever.

A week later the entire crew appeared at 1600 Pennsylvania Avenue NW where President George W. Bush presented the pilot with the Meritorious Service Medal for leadership, and the Air Medal of a burnished eagle in an attack dive clutching two

lightning bolts in its talons overlaid on two metallic overlapping circular discs hanging from a gold-and-blue ribboned chevron to the rest of the crew. In Beijing Premier Jiang Zemin joined the Central Military Commission in praising PLA Finback pilot Wang Wei as a revolutionary martyr and designated him Protector of the Sea and Sky and called him resolute and daring, cool and calm.

But Salinger was not all done here. His cameo in this chapter comes with his verbatim response to this story that got out of hand. In a forthcoming *Paris Review* interview he said W*hat I had left out of the story was a statement made by Vice President Dick Cheney and National Security Advisor Condoleezza Rice, hell, we were just caught and slammed for opening their mail, that's all, even at seventy miles out, well outside the twelve nautical-miles of the international law on territorial boundaries. And besides, they did send us a bill for a two months parking ticket for the Aries at their private Lingshui airport,* which was just enough to save us from using books to wrap barricades around themselves, dancing in our chains.

Maybe because it happened so very fast it was indeed an act of the imagination. Just to be sure, we gather now on Zoom for a wireless confirmation in the eternal imperfect tense so it won't challenge the censors poised with their secret daubers as if they're playing Bingo at the Masonic Lodge. Gotcha or not, it's really *the word forms/on the left; you must stand in line* nevertheless.

[EDITOR'S NOTE: that is the correct translation of what was printed in one of Olson's Maximus poems.]

What follows is a slightly edited transcript of the Zoom conversation, carefully transcribed by our author as part of his contract with redbat books and *The Paris Review.*

Gilbert Sorrentino: *I've been asked to moderate this discussion on the art of fiction. But you must know that since I'm from Brooklyn I can't take this subject seriously.*

Henry James: *However, we must take an active interest which in moments of confidence, we may venture to say a little more what it thinks of itself. We must take ourselves seriously for the public.*

Gertrude Stein: *Now listen! I'm no fool. I know that in daily life we don't go around saying is a...is a...is a. But a rose is a rose is a rose, even here in Paris.*

Percy Lubbock: *Well, that depends on your point of view, no?*

György Lukács: *You must already know that I believe the history of the novel is immersed in transcendental homeless-*

ness, characters longing for utopian perfection. This cannot be spoiled by such modernists as James Joyce or Franz Kafka.

Sorrentino: *I'm surprised you didn't include my name in that last sentence.*

Lukács: *Well, as the minister of culture, I try to be fair and polite to everyone.*

Saul Bellow: *Yes, but not everyone is the same. I am Chicago born and I have taught myself, free-style and first to knock. Sometimes innocent, sometimes not so.*

John Gardner: *But we have to be careful here to be sure that our best work attempts to test human values to find out which is best to promote human fulfillment.*

Agnes Martin: *I'm very careful not to have ideas, because they are inaccurate.*

[EDITOR'S SECOND NOTE: these writers' work includes *The Art of Fiction, The Craft of Fiction, On Moral Fiction, The Theory of Fiction*, and Agnes Martin works in horizontal lines.]

Sorrentino: *What about you, Mr. Cao, seven thousand miles away there in Beijing. Do you need an interpreter?*

Cao Xueqin: *No thank you, my translator is right here in the studio. I believe the novel's words are not just idle description of the everyday world to help the wine down after a meal with friends. From a good writer, those words make human life more real.*

Jorge Luis Borges: *You and I want the same thing, but we approach it so differently. But that makes sense, since we write more than two hundred years and several languages apart.*

Sorrentino: *Can you say a little more about that?*

Borges: *For example, in one of my stories Paul Menard is a French author whose lengthy bibliography begins with a technical article on how the game of chess can be improved by removing one of the rook's pawns.*

But he is best known for immersing himself in seventeenth century Spanish and completely rewriting, line by line, all thirty-five-plus chapters of Don Quixote before tearing up every draft. The story concludes with the suggestion that only a second Paul Menard would be able to exhume and revise those lost pages light years away from social realism.

James: *If I may be permitted to suggest to our august group of distinguished authors, that it might be supposed if I may help myself out with a French word, naïf, that given our world that is so messy and filled with enormous ambiguities and contradictions, we must find our own way to explore it to its fullest extent and enjoy doing so.*

Larry McMurtry: *I don't know about the rest of you, but I try to keep it simple. For me, there are only two worthwhile plots in all of literature: the stranger comes into town, and the stranger leaves town.*

Margaret Atwood: *Except for the true connoisseur who's only interested in the stretch in between.*

Dorothy Parker: *Given this wide range of gaggles, my best gift to a nephew who wants to be a writer is a loaded pistol.*

Sorrentino: *And what about you, Mr. Roth, with glove on and crouched forward at first base in a game in Iowa City.*

Philip Roth: *Sorry to be abrupt, but I have to concentrate on this next batter. He hits to the right, like Tolstoy. It's our*

last chance to end the season with a win. Then I have to go back to continue Libby's story. Sorry.

At this point all the ballots have been filled and the box stuffed.

Sorrentino: *So thank you and that's all folks. Just theme and variations, each chapter bound loosely together by its variation on the same theme. And then there are those like Kafka and Borges; they're on the edge of things and won't take any of this seriously but continue doing what they do best: write.*

Agent, editor, publisher, translator or not, the Zoom conference ended, even though nothing had been confirmed and every line disappeared, real or imagined. Against the best advice of both his publisher and subsidiary agent, in an act of confirmation, the author is insisting on giving the last word to a New Mexico writer.

Simon Ortiz: *If it's fiction, you better believe it.*

Aria called just before the story came out. Politics, he said, politics is what connects everyone to the world around us, but most of the time we are betrayed by their words that have lost their meaning, whose reiteration in the memoirs of their writers become the social glue adhering one generation to another while pledging allegiance to say nothing.

But into this nebula on this side of the Milky Way, someone will occasionally appear and talk to us, whose work will stray from the program and find a new language to disturb the book clubs. One of them is the Han poet and revolutionary of swords and explosives, Qiu Jin, where a statue remembering her can be found at West Lake, outside Hangzhou, China.

Qiu had committed her life to fighting for gender equality and against the Manchus and the ruling Qing government.

漫云女子不英雄，
萬里乘風獨向東。
詩思一帆海空闊，
夢魂三島月玲瓏。
銅駝已陷悲回首，
汗馬終慚未有功。
如許傷心家國恨，
那堪客裡度春風。

Don't tell me women are not the stuff of heroes
I alone rode over the East Sea's winds for ten
thousand leagues
I grieve to think of the bronze camels, guardians
of China, lost in thorns
Ashamed, I have done nothing; not one victory
to my name
I simply make my war horse sweat
So tell me; how can I spend these days here

The Qing government troops finally caught her in 1907 and beheaded her in Shaoxing (30 miles from West Lake) at the age of 31.

A century later, the Han government of the Chinese Communist Party under the presidency of Xi Jinping, incarcerated more than a million Uyghurs, Kazakhs, and Kyrgyz and other Muslims in re-education camps in northwest China near its border with Tibet.

The rest of us had to wait one hundred and eleven years for her words to survive before *The New York Times* would run a belated obituary for Qiu Jin.

It must be about the same for numbers, at least natural numbers, because they cannot be made into symbols, metaphors or parables to confuse us. The use of these numbers in a mathematical trick to tease out the way space curves in field equations of motion actually directed Albert Einstein to a theory about gravitational pull of black holes and a Nobel in 1921. But while much of his work took place at the Prussian Academy of Sciences in Berlin in the 1910s, the actual discovery took place when he accepted a research residency for a couple of years in Brazil in the 2010s when the light from the sun was bent by earth's gravitational pull, causing a warping of the space/time continuum.

When that mammoth 13-million-digit prime number got to Brazil, its president took the key to its capital Brasília and opened the vault to distribute free circus tickets to everyone. Aerialists hung from the rafters of the Rio de Janeiro Opera House and sang their favorite song, cheered on by an overflow crowd of well-wishers larger than the opening for the 2014 FIFA World Cup or the 2016 Summer Olympics. For days, trained zebras and lions that had promised not to attack their trainers accompanied the 7.13 megabyte number through the residential neighborhoods and offered chocolates to those who had flunked high school algebra now gathered at street corners gawking at the long string of hostile digits,

$$2^{43112609} - 1$$

...470,269,330,255,923,143,453,723,949,337,516,054, 106,188,475,264,644,140,304,176,732,811,247,493,069, 368,692, ...

The series started with 2, 3, 5, 7, 11, 13, 17, 19, 23, 29, 31, 37, 41, 47, 53, plump real numbers that can only be divided by themselves and 1. The trumpeting elephant assured us that they form the basic blocks of natural numbers, and don't you forget it. You can't even look up the daily Dow, Nasdaq or S&P 500 without the help of these primes. Competing to keep its readers from defecting to text, tweet, stream, or post, the leading newspaper *Journal de Brasil* conducted a daily contest with a one-million-autographed-Mao-Tse-tung-¥ reward for the first reader to text in the correct number for the daily, three-digit, prime number with the published entry password in Portuguese.

Those with double-liens on their homes had to ante up a spontaneous autobiographical disclosure about their mathematical shortcomings or face closure. Face it, they had failed, in grade school and in high school, and for whatever reason—inattention, had skipped breakfast that day, plain lazy, or just didn't give a shit. Time to ask and tell. Did you fuck up in third grade arithmetic, thereby ending any further learning except to tell time and count change backwards at the checkout register? Can you balance your bank account? Can you tell a Canadian loonie from an American quarter? Can you tell a crow from a raven? And finally, can you tell a Crow from a Blackfeet when they both live on Hollywood Boulevard?

Einstein joined the mathematics professors at the fancy University of São Paulo when they objected to using a network of 75 linked Dell desktop computers at UCLA to generate this new, 46th Mersenne prime number. That's cheating, like asking for divine tutelage. And then you dare come down here dragging that useless twenty-eight mile-long number across the equator behind you, boastful and arrogant? North,

your default orientation, north, that doesn't even exist down here. *Nada, nada.* The knife thrower never misses.

Listen, it's not really that big of a deal, if you have enough computers and enough time and enough interest. We don't even have any use for these numbers past the first thousand that ends in 7919, except for some computation shortcuts in information technology systems that handle vast data streams, and in some code work for government and corporate espionage. And besides, the list of these basic, natural numbers is infinite. Just look at Euler's proof of the infinitude of primes:

$$\sum_{prime} \frac{1}{p} = \frac{1}{2} + \frac{1}{3} + \frac{1}{5} + \frac{1}{7} + \frac{1}{11} + \ldots = \infty$$

By now the patient clown with the red nose and the balloons had time enough to join us and started searching the crowded streets for irony. He found an American hiding in the white space between house numbers holding a winning raffle ticket for a collectible convertible with fins, but he's not sure if the man's from the north or the south, or if he's just lucky. He released the blue balloon on a street corner he can't reveal because he had worked for the CIA in the seventies, just in case. The magician walking besides him coaxed him into letting go of the other balloons as well, and children dashed madly after them, took daring risks, and jumped the gap from rooftop to rooftop over the streets' hard skin below them. They didn't care, they've scraped their knees before, and they were convinced the balloons will give them space for glee and smiles.

In the afternoon the Magic Markers marching band led by Flora Purim and trick riders, accompanied by the Four Mad Mammas who formed a huge quartet of bouncing red capital Ms

stretched across the entry promenade to Rio's Museum of Natural History, projecting sonic joy without any fault in count, pitch, timbre or voice. The dancing in the streets was led again by the president singing and clapping along and giving out babies to same-sex couples until well after midnight. What was not obvious at the time: several digits from the 46th Mersenne prime had taken furlough from the line, and joined the celebration camouflaged as indiscriminate and random letters from the user-friendly alphabet which no one questioned, even when they guessed at the meaning of words they had not seen or heard before or had forgotten. But to this day no one knows for sure the exact location of these digits' point of departure from the line, and if they all returned to their original positions, or if anything had been altered or damaged by their temporary absence. Time will tell, but only with the help of giant primes; if it's going to take some time for this question to be remembered without ambiguity.

Here, however, is where we run into trouble. What is ambiguity? In what language is it articulated? English? Portuguese? What is the mother tongue here? If it's accompanied by irony, it'll definitely complicate these questions. And then what about intention, or symbol, metaphor or parable? Who are you asking, the monkey with the organ grinder, or the dancing bear?

The thing itself or the meaning of the thing? That 19th century Danish thinker had something to say about this, if only our language can capture and retain the thing and its essence and not alter it, or something like that. Maybe the answer lies with numbers, they'll get it right, no doubt about that. But then again, maybe life's more fun with ambiguity, no?

Well you see then, your ticket's all punched out, the show's over for you. If you want to go through this again, you'll just have to follow the number to Argentina to catch its next show. They play better bridge down there. Your Spanish won't be a problem, since you were so good at faking Portuguese here. But don't take my word for it. See that guy there sitting down at the court house steps by the tail end of the number? That's the Ringmaster, and he's taking all this down on a yellow legal pad so we won't forget, see? Go talk to him, he'll tell you if this isn't just another one of those stories we inhabit. Call him Einstein.

History can sometimes be terrifying, and writers trying to write about people who don't understand when their lives are shredded often outsource their work to periodic quotations from a book written by an imaginary author, or from a novel about someone who does not appear in it but who has somehow migrated into a memoir that has appeared on *The New York Times'* best-selling list that readers actually buy and talk about over and over in book clubs all over the country. Is it a novel, or is it a non-fiction, creative or not? Definitely a defying word riddle with no accompanying notes, flat or sharp.

For the subsidiary agent and inexpensive translator contracted to do the work, codes were broken without their knowledge of the target language. Just because the author's name appeared on the cover of the book didn't make it any easier. He didn't even know English. People get touristed in this book business, and the Chinese have an expression for it in the past perfect tense, ***bei lüyou.*** On a calm day without any measurable turbulence, the axial rotation of the sun guarantees that the story was factually based on something that really happened, a phenomena, and that its authenticity can be verified by the spectroscope's analysis of its luminosity even without the assistance of an author or a conductor. A reader does not have to take a cruise to distant ports to find the time to finish reading this book.

See here, he's already looking at Chapter . If we can't remember what that

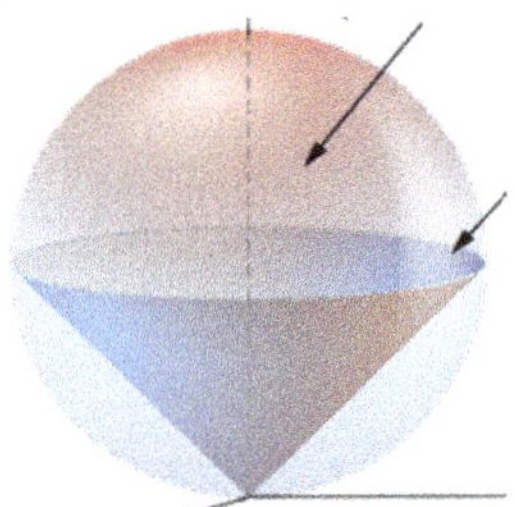

means, we can always turn to Pascal's theorem of the English alphabet for a reminder:

$x^2 + y^2 = z$. But nothing's going on with *z*. Did our author make a mistake? We're having a little geometric problem here. [EDITOR'S NOTE: What Pascal really wrote was an addition of a little superscript *2* to *z* to make it z^2 as in $x^2 + y^2 = z^2$ where for a triangle with a 90° base, the sum of its squared two sides equals the square of the diagonal hypotenuse connecting them.]

It doesn't matter that the English letter *x* is often used by writers, especially journalists, to designate material that needs further investigation or corroboration, or just as a generic substitute for missing but recognizable letters to words unacceptable to the prudent third grade teacher, or as shorthand code for a cabin of words not mentioned between writer and reader, as in Nathaniel Hawthorne's *The Scarlet Letter,* from *a* by Andy Warhol, *G* by John Berger, *S* by John Updike, *V* by Thomas Pynchon, all the way to subversive *Z* by Vassilis Vassilikos.

Alerted by these references then, perhaps they could modify our expectation that a narrative must begin with the cat going up the tree with a middle and end, or that Jack came down without a pail of water and broke his head while Jill came tumbling down and got a shredding from her mother for causing Jack's disaster. Terrifying.

In the competitive world of high level chess matches, this board game that's been around for more than fourteen centuries has acquired symbolic and political significance, like a few other mental or physical games at the international level. Chess is not just chess.

Water polo is not just water polo. The American chess prodigy Bobby Fischer's victory against a field of grand masters at Buenos Aires in the summer of 1971 brought a personal letter from President Richard Nixon: *Your victory brings you one step closer to that world title you so richly deserve, and I want you to know that together with thousands of chess players across America, I will be rooting for you when you meet Boris Spassky next year.* In 2004 Fischer renounced his U.S. citizenship.

If it's true that we are what we read and music is the allegory of our life , who we are can probably be measured and weighed by our favorite games and sports, sometimes leading to the conclusion, ***mene mene tekel upharsin.*** The Russian novelist Vladimir Nabokov, under the name of Vladimir Virin, published *The Defense*, a novel without a single word of dialogue.

In a match to determine who would play the world champion, the main character Aleksandr Luzhin suffers a total mental breakdown just before the beginning of the game and totally fucks up on the first moves of his studied Luzhin Defense against his opponent's pawn-to-king-4 Ruy Lopez opening modified from the Tarrasch Defense.

He spends the rest of his life fixated on developing a chess move that would save him from losing his life, finally disappearing altogether from a high window before someone translated his novel into English, thirty-four years later. And sixty-three years after Nabokov's novel first appeared in Russian, the Italian author Paolo Maurensig published the less-noticed novel *The Lüneburg Variation*, a modernist and suspenseful

story set during the Holocaust of a double chess match between a logical and linear thinking Frisch, a German businessman, and Tabori, a Jew in one of the concentration camps who wins the return match by using an irrational sacrifice of a knight that throws the game into chaos, pushing Frisch into a panic that leads to his losing the game and to his eventual suicide, the same ending for Stefan Zweig's main character in his novella *Chess Story.*

With such focus on world class chess players and their dark side often descending into madness and suicide, it is surprising that readers of these books generally do not mind the detailed technical descriptions of the chess games but will instead forgive the authors for these trespasses. But if an author of a novel that includes the card game of bridge, on the other hand, not only will almost all readers skip the technical descriptions of the game, but they will find the author unforgiveable.

There are few novels with a bridge setting, and Alex Kuo's is one of them. In his novel *Mao's Kisses,* the main character is China's 1989 paramount leader Deng

Xiaoping's main bridge partner and personal notetaker in a story filled with detailed descriptions of the events in Beijing's political spring, as well as bridge tournaments, playing technique, and specific games. His earlier novel *shanghai.shanghai.shanghai*, included descriptions of the actual play of several deals from the 2007 Venice Cup finals held in Shanghai, including a picture of the U.S. winning team holding up an anti-George W. Bush sign made by one of the player's daughter on the back of a dinner menu at the award ceremony in response to the global criticism at their bridge table against their president, reminiscent of the John Carlos and Tommie Smith human rights salute during the 200 meters awards ceremony in Mexico City's 1968 Olympics, resulting in the prompt recall of the entire American track and field team from Mexico. The players on the women's bridge team were at first stripped of all their associations with any sanctioned game in the U.S., which included keeping them from playing professional bridge as well. (After several appeals, these draconian sentences were reduced to months of community service.)

Sports also play a defining role in how a nation sees itself. Until just a few years ago, the three-hour long baseball game has been identified as part of the American DNA. When we want to show what it means to be an American, we take a visitor to a three-hour ball game in which nothing much in the game happens for at least two of those hours, and more than that if the game has strong, dueling pitchers. Besides the major and minor professional leagues, we have the pee wee league, the little league, the Babe Ruth league, and the American Legion league. We enjoy arguing if Duke Snider or Mickey Mantle is a better player, and join Marianne Moore's wish that *Willie Mays should be a Dodger.*

Another writer with Brooklyn connections, Bernard Malamud, wrote a baseball novel *The Natural*, based loosely on the 1919 World Series scandal in which the

2 CENTS Chicago Daily Tribune. FINAL EDITION

BARE 'FIXED' WORLD SERIES

2 CENTS Chicago Daily Tribune. FINAL EDITION

CONFESSES SOX BALL PLOT

2 CENTS Chicago Daily Tribune. FINAL EDITION

TWO SOX CONFESS; EIGHT INDICTED; INQUIRY GOES ON

SECRECY VEILS TERMS OF U. S. SENT TO TOKIO

GRAND AND PETIT MANDATES

ALD. POWERS' HOME BOMBED; POLITICS SEEN

None Hurt; Front of House Wrecked.

Eight Fired by Comiskey; Wrecks Team

"WE THREW WORLD SERIES," CICOTTE, JACKSON, ADMIT

To Indict Gamblers Today Is Plan.

underpaid White Sox players conspired with gamblers and threw the series, leading to the boy's famous lament of Shoeless Joe Jackson, *Say it ain't so, Joe.*

IIn Malamud's novel, Roy Hobbs moves from a star pitcher to the best hitter in the history of the game, especially with his bat, *Wonderboy*, which he made from a tree split

by lightning. But the bat breaks because of Roy's misdeed—like the *Excalibur* in King Arthur's mistake—when he appeared to have accepted a bribe to throw the game, but strikes out anyway in three pitches in the final pennant game, leading a boy to cry, *Say it ain't so, Roy.*

Almost all books that feature baseball lore, real or imagined, are generally uplifting and inspiring and lead to happy endings. Even for the likeable but unlucky schmuck Roy Hobbs, and especially unusually so for Smith in Alan Sillitoe's *Loneliness of the Long Distance Runner,* quite the opposite for those doom-and-gloom novels about chess players.

American sports culture inhabited by these fans is generally very conservative: they are unctuous in their pitch for the national anthem and patriotism; wallow in aphorisms about

life; wax in awe about obedience to authority; do not read more than half a book a year and obliterate the concept of the metaphor in the process of destroying the literacy of their language and its capacity to communicate anything meaningful. Even within such strictures, they also participate in sports gambling, with some ten billion dollars wagered on the college basketball championship March Madness in 2019; they ignore the sexual exploitation of coaches and widespread doping to boost performance; and they deny that sports corrupt American higher education. People like Tommie Smith, John Carlos, Colin Kaepernick and Megan Rapinoe, like the 2007 Venice Cup players, are deemed enemies of the people and often barred from participating in their sport for life. They are waiting to see whose words will survive the damage from the collision of these worlds.

But maybe it all happened so very fast no one knew for sure if was an act of the imagination or the product of what is now acknowledged to be the definitive version written some one hundred years later, this Fritz Kreisler's magical cadenza for Beethoven's violin concerto composed in secret at first, both of them suffering from a hearing loss toward the end of their lives. Such is the pastiche of an unauthorized violin composition project, replacing Beethoven's own furious original that merged the piano and the timpani, much like the project of this novel, whose title had vacillated for months between *Nebulum* and *Cadenza*, finally settling on *Cadenza*s instead of *Cadenze*.

Without form or content, or even any thought of a style to fill the white rectangle of the monitor set at the margins of 1, 1, 1, and 1, and the Georgia font at 12, the project was focused on discovering something without character or plot, and trying to mine something important without a beginning, middle, or end for the serious reader. Without the restraints of content or form, this may as well be written on music paper.

Or the style that stalks every novel, for that matter. Ask Eric Auerbach, Witold Gombrowicz, Primo Levi, Susanne Langer or René Wellek and they might just escape the blabbering on the illusional space between form and content in an imperfect translation, even when James Joyce threw them a sucker punch with his novel about Leopold Bloom in 1922.

Some might say even QE II does a better job when she delivers the Queen's Speech at the annual State Opening of Parliament at the Palace of Westminster, with the 530 carat Star of Africa Cullinan I diamond embedded in the regalic royal scepter, a sign of power, order, and good governance.

As Her Royal Highness sits on the Sovereign's throne and outlines her government's agenda for the coming year, here

the reporter and later the translator of this narrative pauses to disturb the text. There is a potential error lurking about, in either the original reporting or a personal judgment in the interpretation of its meaning.

Does a queen sit on a throne, or does she only appear to be sitting when she is actually perching in order to protect the intricate beadwork of her dress?

Does she make a speech, or does she make a pronouncement, as QE I did in 1588 when she commanded the standardization of the yard and other distances?

And what about the veracity of the translator? Our translator is having her own problems with this project. She has very carefully created an anonymity for herself to protect her neutrality and hence the objectivity of her translations. There is no known photograph of her, which is not that easy today when every smart phone has a locator and a camera. But she also does not have a credit card, making it all the more complicated when she tries to rent a car with cash and a fake driver's license that she bought in Kowloon City's underground market before Hong Kong's return to China in 1997. So far

she has managed to purchase airline tickets through a third party, pay cash for her lodging, and appear in public looking as forgettable as possible, acting as if she's hiding out in some witness protection program.

But now her work is being challenged by her editor, who is claiming that broadcast videos of the same event show QE II saying something entirely different in her speech.

Look at it here, she said, freezing the frame and pointing to it, *this part here*, here's where the queen's Kokoshnik tiara almost tottered off her head when she banged her titanium-tipped Excalibur for emphasis when QE II pronounced, *No more memoirs. I hate memoirs. My people will not be allowed to read memoirs. Never again. And mark these words in stone,* whereupon she banged her Excalibur again.

Yes, but, it was only a draft write-up here, a translation, a cadenza ahead of its time, like a memory of the future, a nebulum.

And what is a nebulum, her editor asked.

Something not bound by time, or words.

The translator is like the writer, she added. Both pitiful spies among all the editors and proofreaders or typesetters that have been left behind. A surveillance team to see if there's any serious writer giving away all the secrets that can be used for suicide, just in case it might just come down to just that since the reader has just been defeated by being exposed to too much fraud.

The line must be getting pretty long by now, the editor added, especially when it includes those wannabe writers wanting to produce best-selling memoirs lined up on the left.

But there is also that other line, that line on the right; but it is getting thin, when these writers are serious about separating what is believed from what is true, and how the censor hidden inside each and every one of us will nudge us to be social and play it safe and say nothing: do not disturb the equilibrium of the republic.

And who are they then, the editor finally asked after a long pause.

That will depend on where we position that line. In the sand? On a map? Inside an idea? On a dare? Here're a dozen, whose politics are grounded in life and not in something as lovely as a tree.

Claribel Alegría
Maya Angelou
Emily Dickinson
Carolyn Forché
Joy Harjo
June Jordan
Maxine Hong Kingston
Carolyn Kizer
Denise Levertov
Audre Lorde
Joyce Carol Oates
Adrienne Rich

At the last recital, a series of notes between the piano and violin collided until the violin's sustained high note toward the end of the sonata's exposition was held for two bars without intervals to interrupt its meaning, clear and significant, as if waiting for an impromptu cadenza or riff without a fermata 𝄐 marking in the score, as if a curtain had been raised to change the program notes forever. Folded into the disgruntled literacy of the state-owned-and-operated telecaster counting the number of people in the concert hall with sandalwood-scented fans, and small opera glasses who had arrived early by Uber or any other consumer pairings of utilitarian interest to corporate sponsors, the two musicians occasionally glanced at each other for any complication in time signature or clarity in note articulation, with the inconspicuous page turner glued to the pianist's left where the line forms, as always.

Both the edited score and the program notes had listed this piece as a violin sonata, directing the casual listener's ear to its slashed and burned quavers at stage center, especially when the violinist was performing on another stolen Stradivarius recently recovered by the F.B.I.

It's also not something one can tap one's foot to, in the beginning, middle or end of this sonata. But in listening to it, or at least most of the time, some of us were slowly assimilating to this language's clichés, even when the writer had fervently rejected them in the first place. These are some of the consequences a writer and a composer have to live with, like it or not. We imagine what we hear, and music becomes the allegory of our life, as if remembering something we did not fully understand, or like this novel that could well end at any

moment, like Joseph Haydn's F#-minor symphony, with the musicians leaving with their instruments, each note decaying one by one in the farewell.

By the time Aria Zoomed back into the meeting, the left half of the monitor showed the orchestral string players who had already completed their tuning standing up to welcome the vocal soloists and the guest conductor to the dais, the distinguished Otto Klemperer, for a performance of Adrian Leverkühn's oratorio, ***Apocalipsis.*** The Milstein sisters—violinist Maria (right) and pianist Nathali—were looking over the score of Vinteuil's violin Sonata in F♮ on the right half of the screen. And we were looking

at the parents of the composers of these two pieces, Thomas Mann in Los Angeles and Marcel Proust in Paris, the authors of *Doctor Faustus* and *Swann's Way*—who had made up the fictional Leverkühn and Vinteuil—standing behind an Aria witnessing everything they had imagined. And yes, Aria, our Aria, he finally looked bewildered in this work of imagination, maybe.

But the ever-inquisitive Milstein sisters were determined to find the real composer behind the imagined Vinteuil when

the imagined sonata performed in the novel included a *little phrase* that *swept over and enveloped* the central character

Charles Swann *like a perfume or a caress.* Like grandparents reversing the ancestry search, they first went through the novel in the original French, word for word, laying out wall maps and charts and entering phrases into their laptops whenever something relating to music was mentioned, and studying the dynamics of every note of the French violin sonatas that were written during this period, trying to imagine what Proust was imagining. Finally they were convinced that he had actually heard a performance of Gabriel Pierné's Violin Sonata in D minor, Opus 36, in some salon in Paris, and which so completely captured his imagination that he remembered and passed its details on to his creation, Charles Swann. And the rest?

Leverkühn's situation is something else altogether. Aria addressed us directly. *Look*, he said, *Mann had lived in Los Angeles too long.* Imagine trying to re-invent Goethe's Faustian theme by having his composer deliberately contracting syphilis in order to inhabit a furious period of mad creativity while trying to escape the wrath of the McCarthy hearings that labeled him a communist. Who's going to perform his

writing? His Schoenberg-like twelve-tone compositions were too much of a threat for the punctual Hollywood Bowl and Disneyland audience, even with the LA Philharmonic in summer residence. For them, Leverkühn and Schoenberg's work would be just noise, one way or another. However, he insisted, ***this was not really a random coincidence.*** In the novel, the premier of Leverkühn's *Apocalipsis* was conducted by Otto Klemperer in Frankfurt, and he was also the conductor of the LA Philharmonic between 1933 and 1939. Mann knew exactly what he was doing when he started writing this novel the year he moved into that modernist house designed for him in the Pacific Palisades suburb of Los Angeles in 1942.

We also knew then that Aria wasn't fooling around. He wanted us to be sure of that, as tenuous and enchanting as the mind and its imagination can be.

When it's not done right, or the reader's placed on the wrong page, the words will be misunderstood by the translator, their idiom having lost its chromatic meaning, especially for the inattentive reader. When this happens, a clinical spectroscopy will show that the novelist, being a creation of his own imagination most of the time, will begin to feel the need to invent new musical instruments to perform his work so that it won't be encumbered by the detritus of the translator and the reader's ideas of things as they are, blue guitar or not. In other words, wrong place, wrong time, maybe a couple of centuries off.

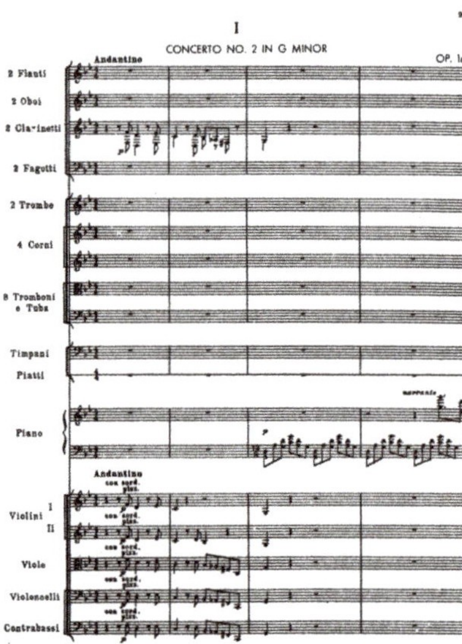

Sergei Prokofiev took a chance when he restructured and rewrote his second piano concerto ten years after the earlier copies were all destroyed in a fire. It is one of the most difficult performance pieces that all but a small handful of pianists today would avoid playing once they are old enough to experience fear and trembling.

The intensity of the crocheted runs with overlapping notes push a ferocious cadenza in double *fortissimo* to take up six minutes, half of the first movement.

The square-jawed and khaki-uniformed archivist director of the National Bibliotica of the Mind in Buenes Aires in Chapter has changed his mind and is now asking the page turner to turn the pages faster as if he were familiar with the score. He knows that the vaults in his library include a copy of the original publication of this second concerto Opus 16 in G minor that had been masked by a faked cataloging system invented by a defrocked librarian who wanted to protect it from Joseph Stalin's wrath, who held his wife and two sons hostage in a Siberian gulag in return for promises to write happy and smiling stories, even while declaring Prokofiev to be an enemy of the people, along with Shostakovich and Khachaturian.

As a dabbling pianist who gracefully accompanies the singers' merriment at family gatherings during the holidays, this archival director who had examined this unknown last remaining 1913 text that had escaped the fire and then completely rewritten from memory after ten years, he is making the final edits of an article that argues for a renumbering of this piano concerto as No. 7—after Prokofiev's incomplete No. 6 for two pianos—because it is substantially different in its content from the currently accepted No. 2, though both appear to be working the exact same form, four movements with the same markings—Andantino-Allegretto; Scherzo-Vivace; Intermezzo-Allegro moderato; Finale: Allegro tempestoso—less foursquare and slightly less precipitous in its contrapuntal fabric, a bit less imaginative in their treatment, perhaps in response to the criticism of its 1913 premier with Prokofiev as the soloist, where one reviewer claimed that cats in the tree make better music.

We now know what the cat did in the tree and why it got up there, at least according to those intentionally clueless historians, scholars and other ideologues. We may also know why Prokofiev and his tormentor Stalin both died in Moscow within one hour on the same March evening in 1953. All of Moscow's winter blooms were usurped for the leader's massive three-day state funeral, preempting any significant remembrance for Prokofiev.

Page turner: translated from the Latin: a book so exciting or gripping that one is compelled to read it rapidly, last seen as the inconspicuous page turner in Chapter , according to our translator, slouched in his chair as if he's waiting for a fermata in

the piano's score to signal the beginning of a cadenza that is not there, at least not in this piece in which Beethoven had paid attention to the sonata form whose content did not leave room for a cadenza even when the high note of the violin held for an extra count at the end of the exposition disrupted the careful meaning of the piano's line, alarming both the pianist and the page turner as well, even though he hid it well inside the blink of an eye. His modus operandi to qualify him for this concert appointment included a cautious and imperturbable personality prepared to be the last to leave the stage in the event of a house fire, and so ordinary in dress and movement

that he would not be noticed to have left the stage before the applause. He would also know the score well, as well as the pianist's preferred time for each individual page turn, especially when it's in the middle of an unusual and complicated run with a 7/8 signature.

The page turner then becomes an author, carefully placing the reader from page to page, like a mannequin whose invisible handler is shaping the words. When it's not done right, the notes from the violin and piano will collide, and the pixels on the page will decay into cosmic dust and breathe memory into another species.

Even a cursory glance at the soloist's first page in the score of Dmitri Shostakovich's Cello Concerto No. 1, would show a simple structure without the nebulous ballots of his Hungarian or Russian contemporaries.

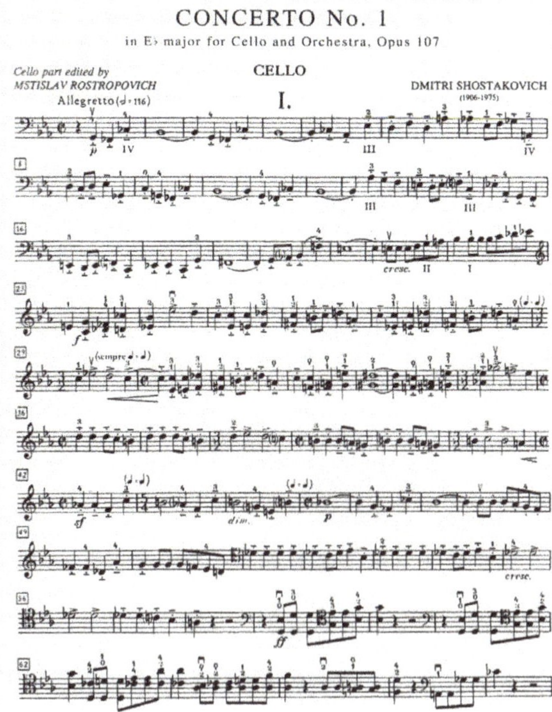

Clear lines of mostly quarter notes and a simple four-note motif that will resonate throughout tomorrow's papers, suggest no need to imagine any malevolent intent.

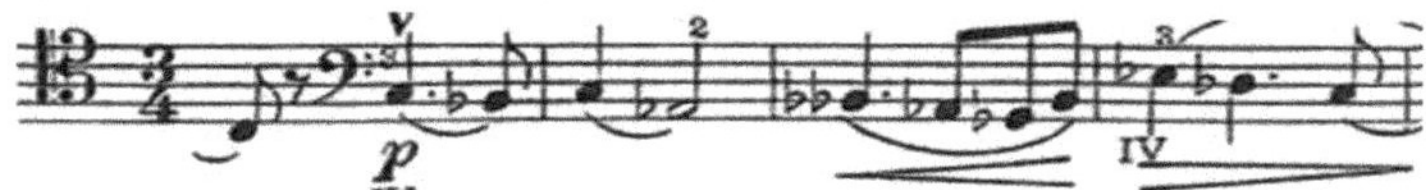

B$^{\flat}$ut then, this is only the opening of a three story serial, four if we count the six minute cadenza. **C**hord progressions are something else altogether.

A$^{\flat}$ria would remind us not to expect the conventional debris of old truths that have taken over our memory. **B**$^{\flat\flat}$elieve me, he said, listen to his chord progressions. **A**$^{\flat}$nd then he added that we are never quite sure what they are all about and how we got here in the first place, but it's always compelling and convincing, like a work of fiction.

G$^{\flat}$ranted that everyone in the room knew it really wasn't fiction at all, we pretended to go along with it anyway. **B**$^{\flat\flat}$ehind every word of Shostakovich's music lurked the possibility of an imminent arrest, maybe a show trial if he were lucky enough, and then marched off to a Siberian work camp, soap and toothbrush in hand. **E**$^{\flat}$xecution was another possibility, after he was declared an enemy of the people, along with Prokofiev and Khachaturian.

D$^{\flat}$edicating this concerto to his good friend Slava Rostropovich, he decided he needed to come up with a new language for this gift. **C**adenza. Preceded by a lower A on the timpani in double *pianissimo,* it'll have be a long one, starting with something quiet and low but in the following six minutes deplete the vocabulary of the cello and run the scale up to the highest pitch on its left string, the A. These six minutes will scoop up all the musical debris left to the side of the first two movements, the loose notes and dropped phrases, as well as parts of our whispered conversations—heard, unheard or imagined—words that have lost their intended meanings,

words that were not meant at all, unfinished sentences, random white noise with no time signature that we use as our social glue to protect us from evil, without which the First Amendment will burn up and we might very well end up in the ninth circle of Dante's inferno.

Believe me, Aria finally said, interrupting again, standing behind the conductor and looking at the text of the cadenza in the teleprompter, granted that the execution of the chord's progressions was even and made sense this time, though they were clearly dedicated to the dominant key. We just sat there and listened, took notes and prepared questions, just before the last seven words in $E^{\flat}$ and double *fortissimo* on the timpani ended and prevented a breathless collision before the applause erupted.

In random notes explaining the characterization of the stories and their inhabitants that are gathered here, some of them are here because they were intentionally requested by the author, some conscripted as walk-ons or cameos just because they were in the neighborhood, some as proxies for uncertain identities just because they were on the nearby bookshelves, and some because they believed their work needs to be represented in this collection, whose dominion yet remains to be sorted out. In any case, they all accepted this assignment seriously, hoping that these words have meaning.

So then the balloting was serious and the result unanimous: Bach's Brandenburg Concerto No. 5 in D, BWV 1050 for flute, violin and harpsichord, with a write-in insisting it really should be renamed as his seventh or eighth keyboard concerto since both the flute and violin have only minimal solo parts compared to the keyboard's long and gigantic solo in the first movement as if Bach were inventing the cadenza for himself as a harpsichordist.

Over the last three hundred years, translators have worked within the galaxy of this cadenza first with quill and ink before moving on to music composition software with 100K memory, and with instruments that pluck, those that use pressurized air, finally settling on those that strike, before going back and trying to acquire some intellectual patent for its domain.

Having lived through the Goldberg Black Pearl Variation 25 in B$^{\flat}$, completed a couple of years before, into this cadenza then, these writers have walked into this novel and this Brandenburg 5 in which notes real and imagined are reproduced and repeated in so many words, they are the only ones left to tell the story.

When there was enough to fill up all the ballots in the room, Aria embraced the particulars and stood up. *Believe me, it all happened so very fast no one knew for sure it wasn't an act of the imagination. Count them,* he repeated, *count them to be sure this isn't something we'll find in tomorrow morning's papers.*

We did just as Aria had asked, signing each piece of paper folding all our promises of secrecy. There was no collusion or dissension.

In a special edition the next morning, the opposition printed their story anyway, and it included specific the names of all the authors who had signed the ballots, including dates. Aria had called just before the story first came out on twitter then later on television. *We have been betrayed; we had all promised to be silent, but someone had betrayed us,* he repeated.

I tried to tell everyone it'll be all right, there was no proof, no corroborating pictures to make the story credible, the republic will not panic.

But Aria reminded us that we didn't have any evidence either—yet we believed they had occurred just like before, much as we often place our trust in random coincidences and wild repetitions and in fact have come to expect them like children—before disappearing entirely, his voice trailing into thin air for the moment.

We continued sitting at the same end of the long conference table trying to reconstruct the details of this book one

by one, repeating them again and again, trying to be sure we had not left anything out, anything at all. There were only five of us left at the end this emergency council meeting.

It was just as he had said, returning at the end, the original manuscript of this novel will be archived in the Natural Bibliotica of the Mind, he announced, along with our ballots.

INDEX

Inscription

Tsien Hsue—Shen (Qian Xuesen), Chinese, 1911-2009
Zoe Filipkowska, Polish, 1946-
Liu Cixin, Chinese, 1963-

A **•_** **1-5**

Charles Olson, American, 1910-1970
Sonny Rollins, American, 1930-
Ludwig van Beethoven, German, 1770-1827
Wolfie Mozart, Austrian, 1756-1791
Richard Wagner, German, 1813-1883
Ralph Carpenter, American, 1943-2011
Miguel del Cervantes, Spanish, 1547-1616
Alex Kuo, American, 1939-
Herman Melville, American, 1819-1891
Cao Xueqin, Chinese, 1715 (1724?)-1763 (1764?)
Wallace Stevens, American, 1879-1955
J.D.Salinger, American, 1919-2010

B **_•••** **6-9**

Ilsa Lund, Swedish, 1915-1982
Johann Sebastian Bach, German, 1685-1750
Wanda Landowska, Polish, 1879-1959
Jeremy Denk, American, 1970-
Tatiana Nikolayeva, Russian, 1924-1993
Igor Levit, Russian, 1987-
Mirjana Lewis, American, harpsichordist, 20th century
John Lewis, American, 1920-2001
Glenn Gould, Canadian, 1932-1952
Verne Edquist, Canadian, piano technician, 20th century

C  _._. **10-11**
Charles Olson
John Cage, American, 1912-1992
Buckminster Fuller, American, 1895-1983
Josef Albers, German/American, 1888-1976
Anni Albers, German/American, 1899-1994
Gwendolyn Knight, American, 1913-2005
Franz Kline, American, 1910-1962
Robert Rauschenberg, American, 1925-2008
Mary Richards, American, 1916-1999
Mere Cunningham, American, 1919-2009
Albert Einstein, German, 1879-1955
William Carlos Williams, American, 1883-1963
Robert Creeley, American, 1926-2005
Robert Duncan, American, 1919-1988
Denise Levertov, American, 1923-1999
Gary Snyder, American, 1930-

D  _.. **12-13**
Miguel del Cervantes

E  . **14-17**
Miguel del Cervantes
Cao Xueqin
Gao E, Chinese, 1738-1815
Rush Limbaugh, American 1951-

R  ._. **18-22**
Jeff Widener, American, 1956-
Mikhail Gorbachev, Russian, 1931-

Deng Xiaoping, Chinese, 1904-1997
Charlie Cole, American, AP photographer
Arthur Tsang Hin Wah, Hong Kong photographer
Stuart Franklin, British, 1956-
Wang Weilin, Chinese, 1970-
George Armstrong Custer, American, 1839-1876
Albert Camus, French, 1913-1960
James Lilley, American, 1928-2009
Cheryl WuDunn, American, 1959-
Nicholas Kristof, American, 1959-
Hou Dejian, Taiwanese, 1956-

O _ _ _ **23-25**

J.G. Ballard, British, 1930-2009

F .._. **26-27**

Charles Olson
Herman Melville

K _._ **28-32**

Dante Alighieri, Italian, 1265-1321
Nicholas III, Italian, 1225-1280
Brunetto Latini, Italian, 1220-1294

G _ _. **33-36**

Elizabeth I, English, 1533-1603
George Washington, American, 1732-1799
Benjamin Franklin, American, 1706-1790
Thomas Jefferson, American, 1743-1826
Minor White, American, 1908-1976

Agnes Martin, American, 1912-2004
Mark Rothko, American, 1903-1970

H **37-38**
Beatrice Portinari, Italian, 13th century
Samuel Taylor Coleridge, British, 1772-1834

N _. **39-42**
J.D. Salinger
George W. Bush, American, 1946-
Jiang Zemin, Chinese, 1926-
Wang Wei, Chinese, @1968-
Dick Cheney, American, 1941-
Condoleezza Rice, American, 1954-

Q _ _._ **43-46**
Charles Olson
Gilbert Sorrentino, American, 1929-2006
Henry James, British, 1843-1916
Gertrude Stein, American, 1874-1946
Percy Lubbock, British, 1879-1915
Gyögy Lukács, Hungarian, 1885-1971
James Joyce
Franz Kafka, Czechoslovakian, 1883-1924
Saul Bellow, American, 1915-2005
John Gardner, American, 1933-1982
Agnes Martin
Cao Xueqin
Jorge Luis Borges, Argentinian, 1899- 1986
Larry McMurtry, American 1936-
Margaret Atwood, Canadian, 1939-

Dorothy Parker, American, 1893-1967
Philip Roth, American, 1933-2018
Simon Ortiz, Acoma Pueblo, 1941-

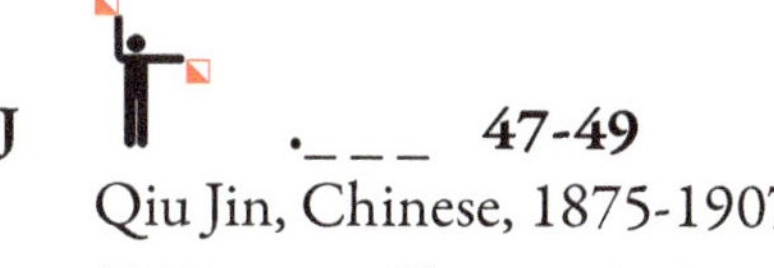

J •_ _ _ **47-49**
Qiu Jin, Chinese, 1875-1907
Xi Jinping, Chinese, 1953-

M _ _ **50-54**
Albert Einstein
Mao Tse-tung, Chinese,1893-1976
Marin Mersenne, French, 17th century
Søren Kierkegaard, Danish, 1813-1855

X _••_ **55-57**
Blaise Pascal, French, 1623-1662
Nathaniel Hawthorne, American, 1804-1864
Andy Warhol, American, 1928-1987
John Berger, British, 1926-2017
John Updike, American, 1932-2009
Thomas Pynchon, American, 1937-
Vassilis Vassilikos, Greek, 1934-

U ••_ **58-61**
Bobby Fischer, American, 1943-2008
Richard Nixon, American, 1913-1994
Vladimir Nabokov, Russian, 1899-1977
Paolo Maurensig, Italian, 1943-
Ruy López, Spanish, 1530-1580
Siegbert Tarrasch, German, 1862-1934

Stefan Zweig, Austrian, 1881-1942
Alex Kuo
Deng Xiaoping
John Carlos, American, 1945-
Tommie Smith, American, 1944-

V ..._ **62-64**

Duke Snider, American, 1926-2011
Mickey Mantle, American, 1931-1995
Marianne Moore, American, 1887-1972
Willie Mays, American, 1931-
Bernard Malamud, American, 1914-1986
Joe Jackson, American, 1887-1951
Alan Sillitoe, British, 1928-2010
Colin Kaepernick, American, 1987-
Megan Rapinoe, 1985-

I .. **65-69**

Fritz Kreisler, Austrian, 1875-1962
Ludwig van Beethoven, German, 1770-1827
Erich Auerbach, German, 1892-1957
Witold Gombrowicz, Polish, 1904-1969
Primo Levi, Italian, 1919-1987
Susanne Langer, American, 1895-1985
René Wellek, Czech-American, 1903-1995
James Joyce, Irish, 1882-1941
Elizabeth II, British, 1926-
Joyce Kilmer, American, 1886-1918
Claribel Alegria, Nicaraguan-Salvadoran, 1924-2018
Maya Angelou, American, 1928-
Emily Dickinson, American, 1830-1886
Carolyn Forchè, American, 1950-

Joy Harjo, Mvskoke, 1951-
June Jordan, American, 1936-2002
Maxine Hong Kingston, American, 1940-
Carolyn Kizer, American, 1925-2014
Denise Levertov
Audre Lorde, American, 1934-1992
Joyce Carol Oates, American, 1938-
Adrienne Rich, American, 1929-2012

L ._.. **70-72**
Ludwig van Beethoven

W ._ _ **73-75**
Otto Klemperer, German, 1885-1973
Maria Milstein, French, 1985-
Nathali Milstein, French, 1995-
Marcel Proust, French, 1871-1922
Gabriel Pierné, French, 1863-1937
Joseph McCarthy, American, 1908-1957
Arnold Schoenberg, German,1874-1951

T _ **76-78**
Wallace Stevens
Sergei Prokofiev, Russian, 1891-1953
Dmitri Shostakovich
Aram Khachaturian

S ... **79-80**
Ludwig van Beethoven

P ·_ _· **81-83**

Dmitri Shostakovich, Russian, 1906-1975
James Joyce
Aram Khachaturian, Russian, 1903-1978

Y _·_ _ **84-85**

Johann Sebastian Bach

Z _ _·· **86-87**

REVIEWS OF ALEX KUO'S WRITING

One of our most gifted and audacious storytellers, who fuses Gone with the Wind, *American missionaries in China, and the 2008 Beijing Olympics to both celebrate and expose the cultural mishaps and hypocrisies of our modern world.*

—AIMEE PHAN

I happen to believe that there are a lot of good poets around at present, but a poet like Alex Kuo, who possesses a highly developed moral sense and a bitter honesty, is rare at any time, and especially in this time. We need him.

—CAROLYN KIZER

The essence of short stories should be: simple and at the same tie profound and disturbing. It is his genius to bring to light now the basic horror of repression, censorship and state terrorism is the same all over the world on any side.

—LUISA VALENZUELA

This fast paced political thriller offers a much needed fresh and multidimensional examination of student unrest on both sides of the Pacific.

—ISHMAEL REED

Alex Kuo is a mainstay of Chinese American and Asian American writing. He has helped to create this field by producing some of its most important work and by defining the field.

—MAXINE HONG KINGSTON

He sculptures lines over minefields of emotions. Very powerful. Incredible silences. I can feel the near explosion, then a dance, a twist to save life. Know what I mean?

—JOY HARJO

redbat
books